THE SOUL-DRINKER

Elric plunged the Black Sword down the demon's stinking throat, wrenching the blade so that it split jaw, neck, chest and groin and the creature's life force began to course along the length of the runesword. The claws lashed out at him, but the creature was weakening.

Then the life force pulsed up the blade and reached Elric who gasped and screamed in dark ecstasy as the demon's energy poured into him. He withdrew the blade and hacked and hacked at the body and still the life force flowed into him. The demon groaned and dropped to the flagstones.

And it was done . . .

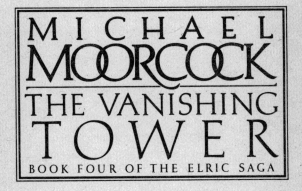

MICHAEL MOORCOCK
THE VANISHING TOWER
BOOK FOUR OF THE ELRIC SAGA

BERKLEY BOOKS, NEW YORK

A version of this novel, re-edited without reference to the author, was
published under the title *The Sleeping Sorceress* by Lancer Books in
1972. The text of this edition follows that of the English edition, published
by New English Library in 1970.

This Berkley book contains the complete
text of the original edition.

THE VANISHING TOWER

A Berkley Book / published by arrangement with
the author

PRINTING HISTORY
Daw Books edition / June 1977
Berkley edition / November 1983
Seventh printing / October 1986

ISBN: 0-425-10171-1

A BERKLEY BOOK ® TM 757,375
Berkley Books are published by The Berkley Publishing Group,
200 Madison Avenue, New York, NY 10016.
The name "BERKLEY" and the stylized "B" with design
are trademarks belonging to Berkley Publishing Corporation.

PRINTED IN THE UNITED STATES OF AMERICA

For Ken Bulmer, who, as editor of the magazine *Sword and Sorcery,* asked me to write this book as a serial for him. The magazine, which was to be a companion to *Visions of Tomorrow,* never appeared due to the backer withdrawing his support from both magazines.

THE VANISHING
TOWER

BOOK ONE

The Torment of the Last Lord

... and then did Elric leave Jharkor in pursuit of a certain sorcerer who had, so Elric claimed, caused him some inconvenience ...

—*The Chronicle of the Black Sword*

CHAPTER ONE

Pale Prince on a Moonlit Shore

  In the sky, a cold moon, cloaked in clouds, sent down faint light that fell upon a sullen sea where a ship lay at anchor off an uninhabited coast.

From the ship a boat was being lowered. It swayed in its harness. Two figures, swathed in long capes, watched the seamen lowering the boat while they, themselves, tried to calm horses which stamped their hooves on the unstable deck and snorted and rolled their eyes.

The shorter figure clung hard to his horse's bridle and grumbled.

"Why should this be necessary? Why could not we have disembarked at Trepesaz? Or at least some fishing harbour boasting an inn, however lowly. . . ."

"Because, friend Moonglum, I wish our arrival in Lormyr to be secret. If Theleb K'aarna knew of my coming—as he soon would if we went to Trepesaz—then he would fly again and the chase would begin afresh. Would you welcome that?"

Moonglum shrugged. "I still feel that your pursuit of this sorcerer is no more than a surrogate for real activity. You seek him because you do not wish to seek your proper destiny. . . ."

Elric turned his bone-white face in the moonlight and regarded Moonglum with crimson, moody eyes. "And what of it? You need not accompany me if you do not wish to. . . ."

Again Moonglum shrugged his shoulders. "Aye. I know. Perhaps I stay with you for the same reasons that you pursue the sorcerer of Pan Tang." He grinned. "So that's enough of debate, eh, Lord Elric?"

11

"Debate achieves nothing," Elric agreed. He patted his horse's nose as more seamen, clad in colourful Tarkeshite silks, came forward to take the horses and hoist them down to the waiting boat.

Struggling, whinnying through the bags muffling their heads, the horses were lowered, their hooves thudding on the bottom of the boat as if they would stave it in. Then Elric and Moonglum, their bundles on their backs, swung down the ropes and jumped into the rocking craft. The sailors pushed off from the ship with their oars and then, bodies bending, began to row for the shore.

The late autumn air was cold. Moonglum shivered as he stared towards the bleak cliffs ahead. "Winter is near and I'd rather be domiciled at some friendly tavern than roaming abroad. When this business is done with the sorcerer, what say we head for Jadmar or one of the other big Vilmirian cities and see what mood the warmer clime puts us in?"

But Elric did not reply. His strange eyes stared into the darkness and they seemed to be peering into the depths of his own soul and not liking what they saw.

Moonglum sighed and pursed his lips. He huddled deeper in his cloak and rubbed his hands to warm them. He was used to his friend's sudden lapses of silence, but familiarity did not make him enjoy them any better. From somewhere on the shore a nightbird shrieked and a small animal squealed. The sailors grunted as they pulled on their oars.

The moon came out from behind the clouds and it shone on Elric's grim, white face, made his crimson eyes seem to glow like the coals of hell, revealed the barren cliffs of the shore.

The sailors shipped their oars as the boat's bottom ground on shingle. The horses, smelling land, snorted and moved their hooves. Elric and Moonglum rose to steady them.

Two seamen leaped into the cold water and brought the boat up higher. Another patted the neck of Elric's horse and did not look directly at the albino as he spoke. "The captain said you would pay me when we reached the Lormyrian shore, my lord."

Elric grunted and reached under his cloak. He drew out a jewel that shone brightly through the darkness of the night. The sailor gasped and stretched out his hand to take it. "Xiombarg's blood, I have never seen so fine a gem!"

Elric began to lead the horse into the shallows and Moonglum hastily followed him, cursing under his breath and shaking his head from side to side.

Laughing among themselves, the sailors shoved the boat back into deeper water.

As Elric and Moonglum mounted their horses and the boat pulled through the darkness towards the ship, Moonglum said: "That jewel was worth a hundred times the cost of our passage!"

"What of it?" Elric fitted his feet in his stirrups and made his horse walk towards a part of the cliff which was less steep than the rest. He stood up in his stirrups for a moment to adjust his cloak and settle himself more firmly in his saddle. "There is a path here, by the look of it. Much overgrown."

"I would point out," Moonglum said bitterly, "that if it were left to you, Lord Elric, we should have no means of livelihood at all. If I had not taken the precaution of retaining some of the profits made from the sale of that trireme we captured and auctioned in Dhakos, we should be paupers now."

"Aye," returned Elric carelessly, and he spurred his horse up the path that led to the top of the cliff.

In frustration Moonglum shook his head, but he followed the albino.

By dawn they were riding over the undulating landscape of small hills and valleys that made up the terrain of Lormyr's most northerly peninsula.

"Since Theleb K'aarna must needs live off rich patrons," Elric explained as they rode, "he will almost certainly go to the capital, Iosaz, where King Montan rules. He will seek service with some noble, perhaps King Montan himself."

"And how soon shall we see the capital, Lord Elric?" Moonglum looked up at the clouds.

"It is several days' ride, Master Moonglum."

Moonglum sighed. The sky bore signs of snow and the tent he carried rolled behind his saddle was of thin silk, suitable for the hotter lands of the East and West.

He thanked his gods that he wore a thick quilted jerkin beneath his breastplate and that before he had left the ship he had pulled on a pair of woollen breeks to go beneath the gaudier breeks of red silk that were his outer wear. His conical cap of fur, iron and leather had earflaps which were now drawn tightly and secured by a thong beneath his chin and his heavy deerskin cape was drawn closely around his shoulders.

Elric, for his part, seemed not to notice the chill weather. His own cape flapped behind him. He wore breeks of deep blue silk, a high collared shirt of black silk, a steel breastplate lacquered a gleaming black, like his helmet, and embossed with patterns of delicate silverwork. Behind his saddle were deep panniers and across this was a bow and a quiver of arrows. At his side swung the huge runesword Stormbringer, the source of his strength and his misery, and on his right hip was a long dirk, presented him by Queen Yishana of Jharkor.

Moonglum bore a similar bow and quiver. On each hip was a sword, one short and straight, the other long and curved, after the fashion of the men of Elwher, his homeland. Both blades were in scabbards of beautifully worked Ilmioran leather, embellished with stitching of scarlet and gold thread.

Together the pair looked, to those who had not heard of them, like free travelling mercenaries who had been more successful than most in their chosen careers.

Their horses bore them tirelessly through the countryside. These were tall Shazarian steeds, known all over the Young Kingdoms for their stamina and intelligence.

After several weeks cooped up in the hold of the Tarke-shite ship they were glad to be moving again.

Now small villages—squat houses of stone and thatch—came in sight, but Elric and Moonglum were careful to avoid them.

Lormyr was one of the oldest of the Young Kingdoms and much of the world's history had been made there. Even the Melnibonéans had heard the tales of Lormyr's hero of ancient times, Aubec of Malador of the province of Klant, who was said to have carved new lands from the stuff of Chaos that had once existed at the World's Edge. But Lormyr had long since declined from her peak of power (though still a major nation of the South-west) and had mellowed into a nation that was at once picturesque and cultured. Elric and Moonglum passed pleasant farmsteads, well-nurtured fields, vineyards and orchards in which the golden-leaved trees were sur-rounded by time-worn, moss-grown walls. A sweet land and a peaceful land in contrast to the rawer, bustling North-western nations of Jharkor, Tarkesh and Dhari-jor which they had left behind.

Moonglum gazed around him as they slowed their horses to a trot. "Theleb K'aarna could work much mis-chief here, Elric. I am reminded of the peaceful hills and plains of Elwher, my own land."

Elric nodded. "Lormyr's years of turbulence ended when she cast off Melniboné's shackles and was first to proclaim herself a free nation. I have a liking for this restful landscape. It soothes me. Now we have another reason for finding the sorcerer before he begins to stir his brew of corruption."

Moonglum smiled quietly. "Be careful, my lord, for you are once again succumbing to those soft emotions you so despise. . . ."

Elric straightened his back. "Come. Let's make haste for Iosaz."

"The sooner we reach a city with a decent tavern and a warm fire, the better." Moonglum drew his cape tighter about his thin body.

"Then pray that the sorcerer's soul is soon sent to

CHAPTER TWO

White Face Staring Through Snow

Lormyr was famous for her great rivers. It was her rivers that had helped make her rich and had kept her strong.

After three days' travelling, when a light snow had begun to drift from the sky, Elric and Moonglum rode out of the hills and saw before them the foaming waters of the Schlan River, tributary of the Zaphra-Trepek which flowed from beyond Iosaz down to the sea at Trepesaz.

No ships sailed the Schlan at this point, for there were rapids and huge waterfalls every few miles, but at the old town of Stagasaz, built where the Schlan joined the Zaphra-Trepek, Elric planned to send Moonglum into town and buy a small boat in which they could sail up the Zaphra-Trepek to Iosaz where Theleb K'aarna was almost certain to be.

They followed the banks of the Schlan now, riding hard and hoping to reach the outskirts of the town before nightfall. They rode past fishing villages and the houses of minor nobles, they were occasionally hailed by friendly fishermen who trawled the quieter reaches of the river, but they did not stop. The fishermen were typical of the area, with ruddy features and huge curling moustaches, dressed in heavily embroidered linen smocks and leather boots that reached almost to their thighs; men who in past times had been ever ready to lay down their nets, pick up swords and halberds and mount horses to go to the defence of their homeland.

"Could we not borrow one of their boats?" Moonglum suggested. But Elric shook his head. "The fisher-

men of the Schlan are well known for their gossiping.
The news of our presence might well precede us and
warn Theleb K'aarna."

"You seem needlessly cautious. . . ."

"I have lost him too often."

More rapids came in sight. Great black rocks
glistened in the gloom and roaring water gushed over
them, sending spray high into the air. There were no
houses or villages here and the paths beside the banks
were narrow and treacherous so that Elric and Moonglum were forced to slow their pace and make their
way with caution.

Moonglum shouted over the noise of the water:
"We'll not reach Stagasaz by nightfall now!"

Elric nodded. "We'll make camp below the rapids.
There."

The snow was still falling and the wind drove it
against their faces so that it became even more difficult
to pick their way along the narrow track that now
wound high above the river.

But at last the tumult began to die and the track
widened out and the waters calmed and, with relief,
they looked about them over the plain to find a likely
camping place.

It was Moonglum who saw them first.

His finger was unsteady as he pointed into the sky
towards the north.

"Elric. What make you of those?"

Elric peered up into the lowering sky, brushing
snowflakes from his face.

His expression was at first puzzled. His brow furrowed and his eyes narrowed.

Black shapes against the sky.

Winged shapes.

It was impossible at this distance to judge their scale,
but they did not fly the way birds fly. Elric was reminded of another flying creature—a creature he had
last seen when he and the Sealords fled burning Imrryr
and the folk of Melniboné had released their vengeance
upon the reavers.

That vengeance had taken two forms.

The first form had been the golden battle-barges which had waited for the attack as they left the Dreaming City.

The second form had been the great dragons of the Bright Empire.

And these creatures in the distance had something of the look of dragons.

Had the Melnibonéans discovered a means of waking the dragons before the end of their normal sleeping time? Had they unleashed their dragons to seek out Elric, who had slain his own kin, betrayed his own unhuman kind in order to have revenge on his cousin Yyrkoon who had usurped Elric's place on the Ruby Throne of Imrryr?

Now Elric's expression hardened into a grim mask. His crimson eyes shone like polished rubies. His left hand fell upon the hilt of his great black battleblade, the runesword Stormbringer, and he controlled a rising sense of horror.

For now, in mid-air, the shapes had changed. No longer did they have the appearance of dragons, but this time they seemed to be like multicoloured swans, whose gleaming feathers caught and diffracted the few remaining rays of light.

Moonglum gasped as they came nearer.

"They are huge!"

"Draw your swords, friend Moonglum. Draw them now and pray to whatever gods rule over Elwher. For these are creatures of sorcery and they are doubtless sent by Theleb K'aarna to destroy us. My respect for that conjurer increases."

"What are they, Elric?"

"Creatures of Chaos. In Melniboné they are called the Oonai. They can change shape at will. A sorcerer of great mental discipline, of superlative powers, who knows the apposite spells can master them and determine their appearance. Some of my ancestors could do such things, but I thought no mere conjurer of Pan Tang could master the chimeræ!"

"Do you know no spell to counter them?"

"None comes readily to mind. Only a Lord of Chaos such as my patron demon Arioch could dismiss them."

Moonglum shuddered. "Then call your Arioch, I beg you!"

Elric darted a half-amused glance at Moonglum. "These creatures must fill you with great fear indeed if you are prepared to entertain the presence of Arioch, Master Moonglum."

Moonglum drew his long, curved sword. "Perhaps they have no business with us," he suggested. "But it is as well to be prepared."

Elric smiled. "Aye."

Then Moonglum drew his straight sword, curling his horse's reins around his arm.

A shrill, cackling sound from the skies.

The horses pawed at the ground.

The cackling grew louder. The creatures opened their beaks and called to one another and it was very plain now that they were indeed something other than gigantic swans, for they had curling tongues. And there were slim, sharp fangs bristling in those beaks. They changed direction slightly, winging straight for the two men.

Elric flung back his head and drew out his great sword and raised it skyward. It pulsed and moaned and a strange, black radiance poured from it, casting peculiar shadows over its owner's blanched features.

The Shazarian horse screamed and reared and words began to pour from Elric's tormented face.

"Arioch! Arioch! Arioch! Lord of the Seven Darks, Duke of Chaos, aid me! Aid me now, Arioch!"

Moonglum's own horse had backed away in panic and the little man was having great difficulty in controlling it. His own features were almost as pale as Elric's.

"Arioch!"

Overhead the chimerae began to circle.

"Arioch! Blood and souls if you will aid me now!"

Then, some yards away, a dark mist seemed to well

up from nowhere. It was a boiling mist that had strange, disgusting shapes in it.

"Arioch!"

The mist grew still thicker.

"Arioch! I beg you—aid me now!"

The horse pawed at the air, snorting and screaming, its eyes rolling, its nostrils flaring. Yet Elric, his lips curled back over his teeth so that he looked like a rabid wolf, continued to keep his seat as the dark mist quivered and a strange, unearthly face appeared in the upper part of the shifting column. It was a face of wonderful beauty, of absolute evil. Moonglum turned his head away, unable to regard it.

A sweet, sibilant voice issued from the beautiful mouth. The mist swirled languidly, becoming a mottled scarlet laced with emerald green.

"Greetings, Elric," said the face. "Greetings, most beloved of my children."

"Aid me, Arioch!"

"Ah," said the face, its tone full of rich regret. "Ah, that cannot be. . . ."

"You must aid me!"

The chimeræ had hesitated in their descent, sighting the peculiar mist.

"It is impossible, sweetest of my slaves. There are other matters afoot in the Realm of Chaos. Matters of enormous moment to which I have already referred. I offer only my blessings.

"Arioch—I beg thee!"

"Remember your oath to Chaos and remain loyal to us in spite of all. Farewell, Elric."

And the dark mist vanished.

And the chimeræ came closer.

And Elric drew a racking breath while the runesword whined in his hand and quivered and its radiance dimmed a little.

Moonglum spat on the ground. "A powerful patron, Elric, but a damned inconstant one." Then he flung himself from his saddle as a creature which changed its shape a dozen times as it arrowed towards him

reached out huge claws which clashed in the air where
he had been. The riderless horse reared again, striking
out at the beast of Chaos.

A fanged snout snapped.

Blood vomited from the place where the horse's
head had been and the carcass kicked once more before falling to the ground to pour more gore into the
greedy earth.

Bearing the remains of the head in what was first a
scaled snout, then a beak, then a sharklike mouth, the
Oonai thrashed back into the air.

Moonglum picked himself up. His eyes contemplated nothing but his own imminent destruction.

Elric, too, leapt from his horse and slapped its flank
so that convulsively it began to gallop away towards
the river. Another chimera followed it.

This time the flying thing seized the horse's body in
claws which suddenly sprouted from its feet. The horse
struggled to get free, threatening to break its own back-
bone in its struggles, but it could not. The chimera
flapped towards the clouds with its catch.

Snow fell thicker now, but Elric and Moonglum
were oblivious of it as they stood together and awaited
the next attack of the Oonai.

Moonglum said quietly: "Is there no other spell you
know, friend Elric?"

The albino shook his head. "Nothing specific to deal
with these. The Oonai always served the folk of Melniboné. They never threatened us. So we needed no spell
against them. I am trying to think. . . ."

The chimeræ cackled and yelled in the air above the
two men's heads.

Then another broke away from the pack and dived
to the Earth.

"They attack individually," Elric said in a somewhat
detached tone, as if studying insects in a bottle. "They
never attack in a pack. I know not why."

The Oonai had settled on the ground and it had now
assumed the shape of an elephant with the huge head
of a crocodile.

"Not an aesthetic combination," said Elric.

The ground shook as it charged towards them.

They stood shoulder to shoulder as it approached. It was almost upon them—

—and at the last moment they divided, Elric throwing himself to one side and Moonglum to the other.

The chimera passed between them and Elric struck at the thing's side with his runesword.

The sword sang out almost lasciviously as it bit deep into the flesh which instantly changed and became a dragon dripping flaming venom from its fangs.

But it was badly wounded.

Blood ran from the deep wound and the chimera screamed and changed shape again and again as if seeking some form in which the wound could not exist.

Black blood now burst from its side as if the strain of the many changes had ruptured its body all the more.

It fell to its knees and the lustre faded from its feathers, died from its scales, disappeared from its skin. It kicked out once and then was still—a heavy, black, piglike creature whose lumpen body was the ugliest Elric and Moonglum had ever seen.

Moonglum grunted.

"It is not hard to understand why such a creature should want to change its form. . . ."

He looked up.

Another was descending.

This had the appearance of a whale with wings, but with curved fangs, like those of a stomach fish, and a tail like an enormous corkscrew.

Even as it landed it changed shape again.

Now it had assumed human form. It was a huge, beautiful figure, twice as tall as Elric. It was naked and perfectly proportioned, but its stare was vacant and it had the drooling lips of an idiot child. Lithely it ran at them, its huge hands reaching out to grasp them as a child might reach for a toy.

This time Elric and Moonglum struck together, one at each hand.

Moonglum's sharp sword cut the knuckles deeply

and Elric's lopped off two fingers before the Oonai
altered its shape again and began first to be an octopus,
then a monstrous tiger, then a combination of both,
until at last it was a rock in which a fissure grew to
reveal white, snapping teeth.

Gasping, the two men waited for it to resume the attack. At the base of the rock some blood was oozing.
This put a thought into Elric's mind.

With a sudden yell he leapt forward, raised his sword
over his head and brought it down on top of the rock,
splitting it in twain.

Something like a laugh issued from the black sword
then as the sundered shape flickered and became another of the piglike creatures. This was completely cut
in two, its blood and its entrails spreading themselves
upon the ground.

Then, through the snowy dusk, another of the Oonai
came down, its body a glowing orange, its shape that
of a winged snake with a thousand rippling coils.

Elric struck at the coils, but they moved too rapidly.

The other chimeræ had been watching his tactics
with their dead companions and they had now gauged
the skill of their victims. Almost immediately Elric's
arms were pinned to his sides by the coils and he found
himself being borne upward as a second chimera with
the same shape rushed down on Moonglum to seize
him in an identical way.

Elric prepared to die as the horses had died. He
prayed that he would die swiftly and not slowly, at the
hands of Theleb K'aarna, who had always promised
him a slow death.

The scaly wings flapped powerfully. No snout came
down to snap his head off.

He felt despair as he realised that he and Moonglum
were being carried swiftly northward over the great
Lormyrian steppe.

Doubtless Theleb K'aarna awaited them at the end
of their journey.

CHAPTER THREE

Feathers Filling a Great Sky

Night fell and the chimeræ flew on tirelessly, their shapes black against the falling snow.

The coils showed no signs of relaxing, though Elric strove to force them apart, keeping tight hold of his runesword and racking his brains for some means of defeating the monsters.

If only there were a spell. . . .

He tried to keep his thoughts from what Theleb K'aarna would do if, indeed, it was that wizard who had set the Oonai upon them.

Elric's skill in sorcery lay chiefly in his command over the various elementals of air, fire, earth, water and ether, and also over the entities who had affinities with the flora and fauna of the Earth.

He had decided that his only hope lay in summoning the aid of Fileet, Lady of the Birds, who dwelt in a realm lying beyond the planes of Earth, but the invocation eluded him.

Even if he could remember it, the mind had to be adjusted in a certain way, the correct rhythms of the incantation remembered, the exact words and inflections recalled, before he could begin to summon Fileet's aid. For she, more than another elemental, was as difficult to invoke as the fickle Arioch.

Through the drifting snow he heard Moonglum call out something indistinct.

"What was that, Moonglum?" he called back.

"I only—sought to learn—if you still—lived, friend Elric."

"Aye—barely. . . ."

His face was chill and ice had formed on his helmet and breastplate. His whole body ached both from the crushing coils of the chimera and from the biting cold of the upper air.

On and on through the northern night they flew while Elric forced himself to relax, to descend into a trance and to dredge from his mind the ancient knowledge of his forefathers.

At dawn the clouds had cleared and the sun's red rays spread over the snow like blood over damask. Everywhere stretched the steppe—a vast field of snow from horizon to horizon, while above it the sky was nothing but a blue sheet of ice in which sat the red pool of the sun.

And, tireless as ever, the chimeræ flew on.

Elric brought himself slowly from his trance and prayed to his untrustworthy gods that he remembered the spell aright.

His lips were all but frozen together. He licked them and it was as if he licked snow. He opened them and bitter air coursed into his mouth. He coughed then, turning his head upwards, his crimson eyes glazing.

He forced his lips to frame strange syllables, to utter the old vowel-heavy words of the High Speech of Old Melniboné, a speech hardly suited to a human tongue at all.

"Fileet," he murmured. Then he began to chant the incantation. And as he chanted the sword grew warmer in his hand and supplied him with more energy so that the eldritch chant echoed through the icy sky.

> *Feathers fine our fates entwined*
> *Bird and man and thine and mine,*
> *Formed a pact that Gods divine*
> *Hallowed on an ancient shrine,*
> *When kind swore service unto kind.*

> *Fileet, fair feathered queen of flight*
> *Remember now that fateful night*
> *And help your brother in his plight.*

There was more to the summoning than the words of the invocation. There were the abstract thoughts in the head, the visual images which had to be retained in the mind the whole time, the emotions felt, the memories made sharp and true. Without everything being exactly right, the invocation would prove useless.

Centuries before, the Sorcerer Kings of Melniboné had struck this bargain with Fileet, Lady of the Birds: That any bird that settled in Imrryr's walls should be protected, that no bird would be shot by any of the Melnibonéan blood. This bargain had been kept and dreaming Imrryr had become a haven for all species of bird and at one time they had cloaked her towers in plumage.

Now Elric chanted his verses, recalling that bargain and begging Fileet to remember her part of it.

> *Brothers and sisters of the sky*
> *Hear my voice where'er ye fly*
> *And bring me aid from kingdoms high...*

Not for the first time had he called upon the elementals and those akin to them. But lately he had summoned Haaashaastaak, Lord of the Lizards, in his fight against Theleb K'aarna and still earlier he had made use of the services of the wind elementals—the sylphs, the sharnahs and the h'Haarshanns—and the earth elementals.

Yet, Fileet was fickle.

And now that Imrryr was no more than quaking ruins, she could even choose to forget that ancient pact.

"Fileet. . . ."

He was weak from the invoking. He would not have the strength to battle Theleb K'aarna even if he found the opportunity.

"Fileet. . . ."

And then the air was stirring and a huge shadow fell across the chimeræ bearing Elric and Moonglum northward.

Elric's voice faltered as he looked up. But he smiled and said:

"I thank you, Fileet."

For the sky was black with birds. There were eagles and robins and rooks and starlings and wren and kites and crows and hawks and peacocks and flamingoes and pigeons and parrots and doves and magpies and ravens and owls. Their plumage flashed like steel and the air was full of their cries.

The Oonai raised its snake's head and hissed, its long tongue curling out between its front fangs, its coiled tail lashing. One of the chimeræ not carrying Elric or Moonglum changed its shape into that of a gigantic condor and flapped up towards the vast array of birds.

But they were not deceived.

The chimera disappeared, submerged by birds. There was a frightful screaming and then something black and piglike spiralled to earth, blood and entrails streaming in its wake.

Another chimera—the last not bearing a burden—assumed its dragon shape, almost completely identical to those which Elric had once mastered as ruler of Melniboné, but larger and with not quite the same grace as Flamefang and the others.

There was a sickening smell of burning flesh and feathers as the flaming venom fell upon Elric's allies.

But now more and more birds were filling the air, shrieking and whistling and cawing and hooting, a million wings fluttering, and once again the Oonai was hidden from sight, once again a muffled scream sounded, once again a mangled, piglike corpse plummetted groundwards.

The birds divided into two masses, turning their attention to the chimeræ bearing Elric and Moonglum. They sped down like two gigantic arrowheads, led, each group, by ten huge golden eagles which dived at the flashing eyes of the Oonai.

As the birds attacked, the chimeræ were forced to change shape. Instantly Elric felt himself fall free. His body was numb and he fell like a stone, remembering only to keep his grip on Stormbringer, and as he fell he cursed at the irony. He had been saved from the beasts of Chaos only to hurtle to his death on the snow-covered ground below.

But then his cloak was caught from above and he hung swaying in the air. Looking up he saw that several eagles had grasped his clothing in their claws and beaks and were slowing his descent so that he struck the snow with little more than a painful bump.

The eagles flew back to the fray.

A few yards away Moonglum came down, deposited by another flight of eagles which immediately returned to where their comrades were fighting the remaining Oonai.

Moonglum picked up the sword which had fallen from his hand. He rubbed his right calf. "I'll do my best never to eat fowl again," he said feelingly. "So you remembered a spell, eh?"

"Aye."

Two more piglike corpses thudded down not far away.

For a few moments the birds performed a strange, wheeling dance in the sky, partly a salute to the two men, partly a dance of triumph, and then they divided into their groups of species and flew rapidly away. Soon there were no birds at all in the ice-blue sky.

Elric picked up his bruised body and stiffly he sheathed his sword Stormbringer. He drew a deep breath and peered upwards.

"Fileet, I thank thee again.'"

Moonglum still seemed dazed. "How did you summon them, Elric?"

Elric removed his helmet and wiped sweat from within the rim. In this clime that sweat would soon turn to ice. "An ancient bargain my ancestors made. I was hard-pressed to remember the lines of the spell."

"I'm mightily pleased that you did remember!"

Absently, Elric nodded. He replaced his helmet on his head, staring about him as he did so.

Everywhere stretched the vast, snow-covered Lormyrian steppe.

Moonglum understood Elric's thoughts. He rubbed his chin.

"Aye. We are fairly lost, Lord Elric. Have you any idea where we may be?"

"I do not know, friend Moonglum. We have no means of guessing how far those beasts carried us, but I'm fairly sure it was well to the north of Iosaz. We are further away from the capital than we were. . . ."

"But then so must Theleb K'aarna be! If we were, indeed, being borne to where he dwells. . . ."

"It would be logical, I agree."

"So we continue north?"

"I think not."

"Why so?"

"For two reasons. It could be that Theleb K'aarna's idea was to take us to a place so far away from anywhere that we could not interfere with his plans. That might be considered a wiser action than confronting us and thus risking our turning the tables on him. . . ."

"Aye, I'll grant you that. And what's the other reason?"

"We would do better to try to make for Iosaz where we can replenish both our gear and our provisions and enquire of Theleb K'aarna's whereabouts if he is not there. Also we would be foolish to strike further north without good horses and in Iosaz we shall find horses and perhaps a sleigh to carry us the faster across this snow."

"And I'll grant you the sense of that, too. But I do not think much of our chances in this snow, whichever way we go."

"We must begin walking and hope that we can find a river that has not yet frozen over—and that the river will have boats upon it which will bear us to Iosaz."

"A faint hope, Elric."

"Aye. A faint hope." Elric was already weakened from the energy spent in the invocation to Fileet. He knew that he must almost certainly die. He was not sure that he cared overmuch. It would be a cleaner death than some he had been offered of late—a less painful death than any he might expect at the hands of the sorcerer of Pan Tang.

They began to trudge through the snow. Slowly they headed south, two small figures in a frozen landscape, two tiny specks of warm flesh in a great waste of ice.

CHAPTER FOUR

Old Castle Standing Alone

A day passed, a night passed.

Then the evening of the second day passed and the two men staggered on, for all that they had long since lost their sense of direction.

Night fell and they crawled.

They could not speak. Their bones were stiff, their flesh and their muscles numb.

Cold and exhaustion drove the very sentience from them so that when they fell in the snow and lay motionless they were scarcely aware that they had ceased to move. They understood no difference now between life and death, between existence and the cessation of existence.

And when the sun rose and warmed their flesh a little they stirred and raised their heads, perhaps in an effort to catch one last glimpse of the world they were leaving.

And they saw the castle.

It stood there in the middle of the steppe and it was ancient. Snow covered the moss and the lichen which grew on its worn, old stones. It seemed to have been there for eternity, yet neither Elric nor Moonglum had ever heard of such a castle standing alone in the steppe. It was hard to imagine how a castle so old could exist in the land once known as World's Edge.

Moonglum was the first to rise. He stumbled through the deep snow to where Elric lay. With chapped hands he tried to lift his friend.

The tide of Elric's thin blood had almost ceased to move in his body. He moaned as Moonglum helped him to his feet. He tried to speak, but his lips were frozen shut.

Clutching each other, sometimes walking, sometimes crawling, they progressed towards the castle.

Its entrance stood open. They fell through it and the warmth issuing from the interior revived them sufficiently to allow them to rise and stagger down a narrow passage into a great hall.

It was an empty hall.

It was completely bare of furnishings, save for a huge log fire that blazed in a hearth of granite and quartz built at the far end of the hall. They crossed flagstones of lapis lazuli to reach it.

"So the castle is inhabited."

Moonglum's voice was harsh and thick in his mouth. He stared around him at the basalt walls. He raised his voice as best he could and called:

"Greetings to whoever is the master of this hall. We are Moonglum of Elwher and Elric of Melniboné and we crave your hospitality, for we are lost in your land."

And then Elric's knees buckled and he fell to the floor.

Moonglum stumbled towards him as the echoes of his voice died in the hall. All was silent save for the crackling of the logs in the hearth.

Moonglum dragged Elric to the fire and lay him down near it.

"Warm your bones here, friend Elric. I'll seek the folk who live here."

Then he crossed the hall and ascended the stone stair leading to the next floor of the castle.

This floor was as bereft of furniture or decoration as the other. There were many rooms, but all of them were empty. Moonglum began to feel uneasy, scenting something of the supernatural here. Could this be Theleb K'aarna's castle?

For someone dwelt here, in truth. Someone had laid the fire and had opened the gates so that they might enter. And they had not left the castle in the ordinary way or he should have noticed the tracks in the snow outside.

Moonglum paused, then turned and slowly began to descend the stairs. Reaching the hall, he saw that Elric had revived enough to prop himself up against the chimneypiece.

"And—what—found you . . ." said Elric thickly.

Moonglum shrugged. "Nought. No servants. No master. If they have gone a-hunting, then they hunt on flying beasts, for there are no signs of hoofprints in the snow outside. I am a little nervous, I must admit." He smiled slightly. "Aye—and a little hungry, too. I'll seek the pantry. If danger comes, we'd do as well to face it on full stomachs."

There was a door set back and to one side of the hearth. He tried the latch and it opened into a short passage at the end of which was another door. He went down the passage, hand on sword, and opened the door at the end. A parlour, as deserted as the rest of the castle. And beyond the parlour he saw the castle's kitchens. He went through the kitchens, noting that there were cooking things here, all polished and clean but none in use, and came finally to the pantry.

Here he found the best part of a large deer hanging and on the shelf above it were ranked many skins and jars of wine. Below this shelf were bread and some pasties and below that spices.

Moonglum's first action was to reach up on tiptoe and take down a jar of wine, removing the cork and sniffing the contents.

He had smelled nothing more delicate or delicious in his life.

He tasted the wine and he forgot his pain and his weariness. But he did not forget that Elric still waited in the hall.

With his short sword he cut off a haunch of venison and tucked it under his arm. He selected some spices and put them into his belt-pouch. Under his other arm he put the bread and in both hands he carried a jar of wine.

He returned to the hall, put down his spoils and helped Elric drink from the jar.

The strange wine worked almost instantly and Elric offered Moonglum a smile that had gratitude in it.

"You are—a good friend—I wonder why. . . ."

Moonglum turned away with an embarrassed grunt. He began to prepare the meat which he intended to roast over the fire.

He had never understood his friendship with the albino. It had always been a peculiar mixture of reserve and affection, a fine balance which both men were careful to maintain, even in situations of this kind.

Elric, since his passion for Cymoril had resulted in her death and the destruction of the city he loved, had at all times feared bestowing any tender emotion on those he fell in with.

He had run away from Shaarilla of the Dancing Mist, who had loved him dearly. He had fled from Queen Yishana of Jharkor, who had offered him her kingdom to rule, in spite of her subjects' hatred of him. He disdained most company save Moonglum's, and Moonglum, too, became quickly bored by anyone other than the crimson-eyed Prince of Imrryr. Moonglum would die for Elric and he knew that Elric would risk any danger to save his friend. But was not this an unhealthy relationship? Would it not be better if they went their different ways? He could not bear the thought. It was as if they were part of the same entity—different aspects of the character of the same man.

He could not understand why he should feel this. And he guessed that, if Elric had ever considered the question, the Melnibonéan would be equally hard put to find an answer.

He contemplated all this as he roasted the meat before the fire, using his long sword as a spit.

Meanwhile Elric took another draft of wine and began, almost visibly, to thaw out. His skin was still badly blistered by chilblains, but both men had escaped serious frostbite.

They ate the venison in silence, glancing around the

hall, puzzling over the non-appearance of the owner, yet too tired to care greatly where he was.

Then they slept, having put fresh logs on the fire, and in the morning they were almost completely recovered from their ordeal in the snow.

They breakfasted on cold venison and pasties and wine.

Moonglum found a pot and heated water in it so that they might shave and wash and Elric found some salve in his pouch which they could put on their blisters.

"I looked in the stables," Moonglum said as he shaved with the razor he had taken from his own pouch. "But I found no horses. There are signs, however, that some beasts have been kept there recently."

"There is only one other way to travel," Elric said. "There might be skis somewhere in the castle. It is the sort of thing you might expect to find, for there is snow in these parts for at least half the year. Skis would speed our progress back towards Iosaz. As would a map and a lodestone if we could find one."

Moonglum agreed. "I'll search the upper levels." He finished his shaving, wiped his razor and replaced it in his pouch.

Elric got up. "I'll go with you."

Through the empty rooms they wandered, but they found nothing.

"No gear of any kind." Elric frowned. "And yet there is a strong sense that the castle *is* inhabited—and evidence, too, of course."

They searched two more floors and there was not even dust in the rooms.

"Well, perhaps we walk after all," Moonglum said in resignation. "Unless there was wood with which we could manufacture skis of some kind. I might have seen some in the stables. . . ."

They had reached a narrow stair which wound up the highest tower of the castle.

"We'll try this and then count our quest unsuccessful," Elric said.

And so they climbed the stair and came to a door at

the top which was half-open. Elric pushed it back and then he hesitated.

"What is it?" Moonglum, who was below him, asked.

"This room is furnished," Elric said quietly.

Moonglum ascended two more steps and peered round Elric's shoulder. He gasped.

"And occupied!"

It was a beautiful room. Through crystal windows came pale light which sparkled and fell on hangings of many-coloured silk, on embroidered carpets and tapestries of hues so fresh they might have been made only a moment before.

In the centre of this room was a bed, draped in ermine, with a canopy of white silk.

And on the bed lay a young woman.

Her hair was black and it shone. Her gown was of the deepest scarlet. Her limbs were like rose-tinted ivory and her face was very fair, the lips slightly parted as she breathed.

She was asleep.

Elric took two steps towards the woman on the bed and then he stopped suddenly. He was shuddering. He turned away.

Moonglum was alarmed. He saw bright tears in Elric's crimson eyes.

"What is it, friend Elric?"

Elric moved his white lips but was incapable of speech. Something like a groan came from his throat.

"Elric. . . ."

Moonglum placed a hand on his friend's arm. Elric shook it off.

Slowly the albino turned again towards the bed, as if forcing himself to behold an impossibly horrifying sight. He breathed deeply, straightening his back and resting his left hand on the pommel of his sorcerous blade.

"Moonglum. . . ."

He was forcing himself to speak. Moonglum glanced at the woman on the bed, glanced at Elric. Did he recognise her?

"Moonglum—this is a sorcerous sleep. . . ."

"How know you that?"

"It—it is a similar slumber to that in which my cousin Yyrkoon put my Cymoril. . . ."

"Gods! Think you that. . . ?"

"I think nothing!"

"But it is not—"

"—it is not Cymoril. I know. I—she is like her—so like her. But unlike her, too. . . . It is only that I could not have expected. . . ."

Elric bowed his head.

He spoke in a low voice. "Come, let's be gone from here."

"But she must be the owner of this castle. If we awakened her we could—"

"She cannot be awakened by such as we. I told you, Moonglum. . . ." Elric drew another deep breath. "It is an enchanted sleep she is in. I could not wake Cymoril from it, with all my powers of sorcery. Unless one has certain magical aids, some knowledge of the exact spell used, there is nothing that can be done. Quickly, Moonglum, let us depart."

There was an edge to Elric's voice which made Moonglum shiver.

"But . . ."

"Then I will go!"

Elric almost ran from the room. Moonglum heard his footsteps echoing rapidly down the long staircase.

He went up to the sleeping woman and stared down at her beauty.

He touched the skin. It was unnaturally cold. He shrugged and made to leave the chamber, pausing for a moment only to notice that a number of ancient battle-shields and weapons hung on one wall of the room, behind the bed. Strange trophies with which a beautiful woman should wish to decorate her bedroom, he thought. He saw the carved wooden table below the trophies. Something lay upon it. He stepped back into the room. A peculiar sensation filled him as he saw that it was a map. The castle was marked and so was the Zaphra-Trepek river.

Holding the map down to the table was a lodestone, set in silver on a long silver chain.

He grabbed the map in one hand and the lodestone in the other and ran from the room.

"Elric! Elric!"

He raced down the stairs and reached the hall. Elric had gone. The door of the hall was open.

He followed the albino out of the mysterious castle and into the snow.

"Elric!"

Elric turned, his face set and his eyes tormented.

Moonglum showed him the map and the lodestone.

"We are saved, after all, Elric!"

Elric looked down at the snow. "Aye. So we are."

CHAPTER FIVE

Doomed Lord Dreaming

And two days later they reached the upper reaches of the Zaphra-Trepek and the trading town of Alorasaz with its towers of finely carved wood and its beautifully made timber houses.

To Alorasaz came the fur trappers and the miners, the merchants from Iosaz, downriver, or from afar as Trepesaz on the coast. A cheerful, bustling town with its streets lit and heated by great, red braziers at every corner. These were tended by citizens specially commissiond to keep them burning hot and bright. Wrapped in thick woollen clothing, they hailed Elric and Moonglum as they entered the city.

For all they had been sustained by the wine and meat Moonglum had thought to bring, they were weary from their walk across the steppe.

They made their way through the rumbustious crowd —laughing, red-cheeked women and burly, fur-swathed men whose breath steamed in the air, mingling with the smoke from the braziers, as they took huge swallows from gourds of beer or skins of wine, conducting their business with the slightly less bucolic merchants of the more sophisticated townships.

Elric was looking for news and he knew that if he found it anywhere it would be in the taverns. He waited while Moonglum followed his nose to the best of Alorasaz's inns and came back with the news of where it could be found.

They walked a short distance and entered a rowdy tavern crammed with big, wooden tables and benches on which were jammed more traders and more merchants

all arguing cheerfully, holding up furs to display their
quality or to mock their worthlessness, depending on
which point of view was taken.

Moonglum left Elric standing in the doorway and
went to speak with the landlord, a hugely fat man with
a glistening scarlet face.

Elric saw the landlord bend and listen to Moonglum.
The man nodded and raised an arm to bellow at Elric
to follow him and Moonglum.

Elric inched his way through the press and was
knocked half off his feet by a gesticulating trader who
apologised cheerfully and profusely and offered to buy
him a drink.

"It is nothing," Elric said faintly.

The man got up. "Come on, sir, it was my fault. . . ."
His voice tailed off as he saw the albino's face. He
mumbled something and sat down again, making a wry
remark to one of his companions.

Elric followed Moonglum and the landlord up a
flight of swaying wooden stairs, along a landing and
into a private room which, the landlord told them, was
all that was available.

"Such rooms as these are expensive during the winter
market," the landlord said apologetically.

And Moonglum winced as, silently, Elric handed the
man another precious ruby worth a small fortune.

The landlord looked at it carefully and then laughed.
"This inn will have fallen down before your credit's up,
master. I thank thee. Trading must be good this sea-
son! I'll have drink and viands sent up at once!"

"The finest you have, landlord," said Moonglum, trying to make the best of things.

"Aye—I wish I had better."

Elric sat down on one of the beds and removed his
cloak and his sword-belt. The chill had not left his
bones.

"I wish you would give me charge of our wealth,"
Moonglum said as he removed his boots by the fire.
"We might have need of it before this quest is ended."

But Elric seemed not to hear him.

After they had eaten and discovered from the landlord that a ship was leaving the day after tomorrow for
Iosaz, Elric and Moonglum went to their separate beds
to sleep.

Elric's dreams were troubled that night. More than
usual did phantoms come to walk the dark corridors of
his mind.

He saw Cymoril screaming as the Black Sword drank
her soul. He saw Imrryr burning, her fine towers crum-
bling. He saw his cackling cousin Yyrkoon sprawling on
the Ruby Throne. He saw other things which could not
possibly be part of his past. . . .

Never quite suited to be ruler of the cruel folk of
Melniboné, Elric had wandered the lands of men only
to discover that he had no place there, either. And in
the meantime Yyrkoon had usurped the kingship, had
tried to force Cymoril to be his and, when she refused,
put her into a deep and sorcerous slumber from which
only he could wake her.

Now Elric dreamed that he had found a Nanorion,
the mystic gem which could awaken even the dead. He
dreamed that Cymoril was still alive, but sleeping, and
that he placed the Nanorion on her forehead and that
she woke up and kissed him and left Imrryr with him,
sailing through the skies on Flamefang, the great Melnibonéan battle dragon, away to a peaceful castle in the
snow.

He awoke with a start.

It was the dead of night.

Even the noise from the tavern below had subsided.

He opened his eyes and saw Moonglum fast asleep
in the next bed.

He tried to return to sleep, but it was impossible. He
was sure that he could sense another presence in the
room. He reached out and gripped the hilt of Stormbringer, prepared to defend himself should any attackers
strike at him. Perhaps it was thieves who had heard of
his generosity towards the innkeeper?

He heard something move in the room and, again, he
opened his eyes.

She was standing there, her black hair curling over her shoulders, her scarlet gown clinging to her body. Her lips curved in a smile of irony and her eyes regarded him steadily.

She was the woman he had seen in the castle. The sleeping woman. Was this part of the dream?

"Forgive me for thus intruding upon your slumber and your privacy, my lord, but my business is urgent and I have little time to spare."

Elric saw that Moonglum still slept as if in a drugged slumber.

He sat upright in his bed. Stormbringer moaned softly and then was silent.

"You seem to know me, my lady, but I do not—"

"I am called Myshella. . . ."

"Empress of the Dawn?"

She smiled again. "Some have named me that. And others have called me the Dark Lady of Kaneloon."

"Whom Aubec loved? Then you must have preserved your youth carefully, Lady Myshella."

"No doing of mine. It is possible that I am immortal. I do not know. I know only one thing and that is that Time is a deception. . . ."

"Why do you come?"

"I cannot stay for long. I come to seek your aid."

"In what way?"

"We have an enemy in common, I believe."

"Theleb K'aarna?"

"The same."

"Did he place that enchantment upon you that made you sleep?"

"Aye."

"And he sent his Oonai against me. That is how—"

She raised her hand.

"I sent the chimeræ to find you and bring you to me. They meant you no harm. But it was the only thing I could do, for Theleb K'aarna's spell was already beginning to work. I battle his sorcery, but it is strong and I am unable to revive myself for more than very short periods. This is one such period. Theleb K'aarna has joined forces with Prince Umbda, Lord of the Kelmain Hosts. Their plan is to conquer Lormyr and, ultimately, the entire Southern world!"

"Who is this Umbda? I have heard neither of him nor of the Kelmain Hosts. Some noble of Iosaz, perhaps, who . . ."

"Prince Umbda serves Chaos. He comes from the lands beyond World's Edge and his Kelmain are not men at all, though they have the appearance of men."

"So Theleb K'aarna was in the far south, after all."

"That is why I came to you tonight."

"You wish me to help you?"

"We both need Theleb K'aarna destroyed. His sorcery is what enabled Prince Umbda to cross World's Edge. Now that sorcery is strengthened by what Umbda brings—the friendship of Chaos. I protect Lormyr and I serve Law. I know that you serve Chaos, yet I hope your hatred of Theleb K'aarna overcomes that loyalty for the moment."

"Chaos has not served me, of late, lady, so I'll forget that loyalty. I would have my vengeance on Theleb K'aarna and if we can help each other in the matter, so much the better."

"Good."

She gasped then and her eyes glazed. When next she spoke it was with some difficulty.

"The enchantment is exerting its hold again. I have a steed for you near the town's north gate. It will bear you to an island in the Boiling Sea. On that island is a palace called Ashaneloon. It is there that I have dwelt of late, until I sensed Lormyr's danger . . ."

She pressed her hand to her brow and swayed.

". . . But Theleb K'aarna expected me to try to return there and he placed a guardian at the palace's gate. That guardian must be destroyed. When you have destroyed it you must go to the . . ."

Elric rose to help her, but she waved him away.

". . . to the eastern tower. In the tower's lower room is a chest. In the chest is a large pouch of cloth-of-gold. You must take that and—and bring it back to Kaneloon, for Umbda and his Kelmain now march against the castle. Theleb K'aarna will destroy the castle with their help—and destroy me, also. With the pouch, I may destroy them. But pray that I am able to wake, or the South is doomed and even you will not be able to go against the power that Theleb K'aarna will wield."

"What of Moonglum?" Elric glanced at his sleeping friend. "Can he accompany me?"

"Best not. Besides, he has a light enchantment upon him. There is no time to wake him. . . ." She gasped again and flung her arms across her forehead. "No time. . . ."

Elric leaped from the bed and began to pull on his breeks. He took his cloak from where it was draped across a stool and he buckled on his runesword. He went forward to help her, but she signalled him away.

"No. . . . Go, please. . . ."

And she vanished.

Still half asleep Elric flung open the door and dashed down the stairs, out into the night, racing for the north gate of Alorosaz, passing through it and running on through the snow, looking this way and that. The cold flooded over him like a sudden wave. He was soon knee-deep in snow. Peering about him he carried on until he stopped in his tracks.

He gasped in astonishment when he saw the steed which Myshella had provided for him.

"What's this? Another chimera?"

He approached it cautiously.

CHAPTER SIX

Jewelled Bird Speaking

It was a bird, but it was not a bird of flesh and blood.

It was a bird of silver and of gold and of brass. Its wings clashed as he approached it and it moved its huge clawed feet impatiently, turning cold, emerald eyes to regard him.

On its back was a saddle of carved onyx chased in gold and copper and the saddle was empty, awaiting him.

"Well, I began all this unquestioningly," Elric said to himself. "I might as well complete it in the same manner."

And he went up to the bird and he climbed up its side and he lowered himself somewhat cautiously into the saddle.

The wings of gold and silver flapped with the sound of a hundred cymbals meeting and with three movements had taken the bird of metal and its rider high up into the night sky above Alorosaz. It turned its bright head on its neck of brass and it opened its curved beak of gem-studded steel.

"Well, master, I am commanded to take thee to Ashanaloon."

Elric waved a pale hand. "Wherever you will. I am at the mercy of you and your mistress."

And then he was jerked backward in the saddle as the bird's wings beat the stronger and it gathered speed and he was rushing through the freezing night, over snowy plains, over mountains, over rivers, until the coast came in sight and he saw the sea in the west which was called the Boiling Sea.

Down through the pitch blackness dropped the bird of gold and silver and now Elric felt damp heat strike his face and hands, heard a peculiar bubbling sound, and he knew they were flying over that strange sea said to be fed by volcanoes lying deep below its surface, a sea where no ships sailed.

Steam surrounded them now. Its heat was almost unbearable, but through it Elric began to make out the silhouette of a landmass, a small rocky island on which stood a single building and slender towers and turrets and domes.

"The palace of Ashaneloon," said the bird of silver and gold. "I will alight among the battlements, master, but I fear that thing you must meet before our errand is accomplished, so I will await you elsewhere. Then, if you live, I will return to take you back to Kaneloon. And, if you die, I will go back to tell my mistress of your failure."

Over the battlements the bird now hovered, its wings beating, and Elric reflected that there would be no advantage of surprise over whatever it was the bird feared so much.

He swung one leg from the saddle, paused, and then leapt down to the flat roof.

Hastily the bird retreated into the black sky.

Elric was alone.

All was silent, save for the drumming of warm waves on a distant shore.

He located the eastern tower and began to make his way towards the door. There was some chance, perhaps, that he could complete his quest without the necessity of facing the palace's guardian.

But then a monstrous bellow sounded behind him and he wheeled, knowing that this must be the guardian. A creature stood there, its red-rimmed eyes full of insensate malice.

"So you are Theleb K'aarna's slave," said Elric. He reached for Stormbringer and the sword seemed to spring into his hand at its own volition. "Must I kill you, or will you be gone now?"

The creature bellowed again, but it did not move.

The albino said: "I am Elric of Melniboné, last of a line of great sorcerer kings. This blade I wield will do more than kill you, friend demon. It will drink your soul and feed it to me. Perhaps you have heard of me by another name? By the name of the Soul Thief?"

The creature lashed its serrated tail and its bovine nostrils distended. The horned head swayed on the short neck and the long teeth gleamed in the darkness. It reached out scaly claws and began to lumber towards the Prince of Ruins.

Elric took the sword in both hands and spread his feet wide apart on the flagstones and prepared to meet the monster's charge. Foul breath struck his face. Another bellow and then it was upon him.

Stormbringer howled and spilled black radiance over both. The runes carved in the blade glowed with a greedy glow as the thing of Hell slashed at Elric's body with its claws, ripping the shirt from him and baring his chest.

The sword came down.

The demon roared as the scales of its shoulder received the blow but did not part. It danced to one side and attacked again. Elric swayed back, but now a thin wound was opened in his arm from elbow to wrist.

Stormbringer struck for the second time and hit the demon's snout so that it shrieked and lashed out once more. Again its claws found Elric's body and blood smeared his chest from a shallow cut.

Elric fell back, losing his footing on the stones. He almost went down, but recovered his balance and defended himself as best he could. The claws slashed at him, but Stormbringer drove them to one side.

Elric began to pant and the sweat poured down his face and he felt desperation well in him and then that desperation took a different quality and his eyes glowed and his lips snarled.

"Know you that I am Elric!" he cried. "Elric!"

Still the creature attacked.

"I am Elric—more demon than man! Begone, you ill-shaped thing!"

The creature bellowed and pounced and this time Elric did not fall back, but, his face writhing in terrible rage, reversed his grip on the runesword and plunged it point first into the demon's open jaws.

He plunged the Black Sword down the stinking throat, down into the torso.

He wrenched the blade so that it split jaw, neck, chest and groin and the creature's life force began to course along the length of the runesword. The claws lashed out at him, but the creature was weakening.

Then the life force pulsed up the blade and reached Elric who gasped and screamed in dark ecstasy as the demon's energy poured into him. He withdrew the blade and hacked and hacked at the body and still the life-force flowed into him and gave greater power to his blows. The demon groaned and dropped to the flagstones.

And it was done.

And a white-faced demon stood over the dead thing of Hell and its crimson eyes blazed and its pale mouth opened and it roared with wild laughter, flinging its arms upward, the runesword flaming with a black and horrid flame, and it howled a wordless, exultant song to the Lords of Chaos.

There was silence suddenly.

And then it bowed its head and it wept.

Now Elric opened the door to the eastern tower and stumbled through absolute blackness until he came to the lowest room. The door to the room was locked and barred, but Stormbringer smashed through it and the Last Lord of Melniboné entered a lighted room in which squatted a chest of iron.

His sword sundered the bands securing the chest and he flung open the lid and saw that there were many wonders in the chest, as well as the pouch made from cloth-of-gold, but he picked out only the pouch and tucked it into his belt as he raced from the room, back to the battlements where the bird of silver and gold stood pecking with its steel beak at the remnants of Theleb K'aarna's servant.

It looked up as Elric returned. In its eyes was an expression almost of humour.

"Well, master, we must make haste to Kaneloon."

"Aye."

Nausea had begun to fill Elric. His eyes were gloomy as he contemplated the corpse and that which he had stolen from it. Such life force, whatever else it was, must surely be tainted. Did not he drink something of the demon's evil when his sword drank its soul?

He was about to climb back into the onyx saddle when he saw something gleaming amongst the black and yellow entrails he had spilled. It was the demon's heart—an irregularly shaped stone of deep blue and purple and green. It still pulsed, though its owner was dead.

Elric stooped and picked it up. It was wet and so hot that it almost burned his hand, but he tucked it into his pouch, then mounted the bird of silver and gold.

His bone-white face flickered with a dozen strange emotions as he let the bird bear him back over the Boiling Sea. His milk-white hair flew wildly behind him and he was oblivious of the wounds on his arm and chest.

He was thinking of other things. Some of his thoughts lay in the past and others were in the future. And he laughed bitterly twice and his eyes shed tears and he spoke once.

"Ah, what agony is this Life!"

CHAPTER SEVEN

Black Wizard Laughing

       To Kaneloon they came in the early dawn and in the distance Elric saw a massive army darkening the snow and he knew it must be the Kelmain Host, led by Theleb K'aarna and Prince Umbda, marching against the lonely castle.

The bird of gold and silver flapped down in the snow outside the castle's entrance and Elric dismounted. Then the bird had risen into the air again and was gone.

The great gate of Castle Kaneloon was closed this time and he gathered his tattered cloak about his naked torso and he hammered on the gate with his fists and he forced a cry from his dry lips.

"Myshella! Myshella!"

There was no answer.

"Myshella! I have returned with that which you need!"

He feared she must have fallen into her enchanted slumber again. He looked towards the south and the dark tide had rolled a little closer to the castle.

"Myshella!"

Then he heard a bar being drawn and the gates groaned open and there stood Moonglum, his face strained and his eyes full of something of which he could not speak.

"Moonglum! How came you here?"

"I know not how, Elric." Moonglum stepped aside so that Elric could enter. He replaced the bar. "I lay in my bed last night when a woman came to me—the same woman we saw, sleeping, here. She said I must go with her. And somehow go I did. But I know not how, Elric. I know not how."

"And where is that woman?"

"Where we first saw her. She sleeps and I cannot wake her."

Elric drew a deep breath and told, briefly, what he knew of Myshella and the host that came against her Castle Kaneloon.

"Do you know the contents of that pouch?" Moonglum asked.

Elric shook his head and opened the pouch to peer inside. "It seems to be nothing but a pinkish dust. Yet it must be some powerful sorcery if Myshella believes it can defeat the entire Kelmain Host."

Moonglum frowned. "But surely Myshella must work the charm herself if only she knows what it is?"

"Aye."

"And Theleb K'aarna has enchanted her."

"Aye."

"And now it is too late, for Umbda—whoever he may be—nears the castle."

"Aye." Elric's hand trembled as he drew from his belt the thing he had taken from the demon just before he left the Palace of Ashaneloon. "Unless this is the stone I think it is."

"What is that?"

"I know a legend. Some demons possess these stones as hearts." He held it to the light so that the blues and purples and greens writhed. "I have never seen one, but I believe it to be the thing I once sought for Cymoril when I tried to lift my cousin's charm from her. What I sought but never found was a Nanorion. A stone of magical powers said to be able to waken the dead—or those in deathlike sleep."

"And that is a Nanorion. It will awaken Myshella?"

"If anything can, then this will, for I took it from Theleb K'aarna's own demon and that must improve the efficaciousness of the magic. Come." Elric strode through the hall and up the stairs until he came to Myshella's room where she lay, as he had seen her before, on the bed hung with draperies, her wall hung with shields and weapons.

"Now I understand why these arms decorate her chamber," Moonglum said. "According to legend, these are the shields and weapons of all those who loved Myshella and championed her cause."

Elric nodded and said, as if to himself, "Aye, she was ever an enemy of Melniboné was the Empress of the Dawn."

He held the pulsing stone delicately and reached out to place it on her forehead.

"It makes no difference," Moonglum said after a moment. "She does not stir."

"There is a rune, but I remember it not. . . ." Elric pressed his fingers to his temples. "I remember it not. . . ."

Moonglum went to the window. "We can ask Theleb K'aarna, perhaps," he said ironically. "He will be here soon enough."

Then Moonglum saw that there were tears again in Elric's eyes and that he had turned away, hoping Moonglum would not see. Moonglum cleared his throat. "I have some business below. Call me if you should require my help."

He left the room and closed the door and Elric was alone with the woman who seemed, increasingly, a dreadful phantom from his most frightful dreams.

He controlled his feverish mind and tried to discipline it, to remember the crucial runes in the High Speech of Old Melniboné.

"Gods!" he hissed. "Help me!"

But he knew that in this matter in particular the Lords of Chaos would not assist him—would hinder him if they could, for Myshella was one of the chief instruments of Law upon the Earth, had been responsible for driving Chaos from the world.

He fell to his knees beside her bed, his hands clenched, his face twisting with the effort.

And then it came back to him. His head still bent, he stretched out his right hand and touched the pulsing stone, stretched out his left hand and rested it upon Myshella's navel, and he began a chant in an ancient tongue that had been spoken before true men had ever walked the Earth. . . .

"Elric!"

Moonglum burst into the room and Elric was wrenched from his trance.

"Elric! We are invaded! Their advance riders. . . ."

"What?"

"They have broken into the castle—a dozen of them. I fought them off and barred the way up to this tower, but they are hacking at the door now. I think they have been sent to destroy Myshella if they could. They were surprised to discover me here."

Elric rose and looked carefully down at Myshella. The rune was finished and had been repeated almost through again when Moonglum had come in. She did not stir yet.

"Theleb K'aarna worked his sorcery from a distance," Moonglum said. "Ensuring that Myshella would not resist him. But he did not reckon with us."

He and Elric hurried from the room, down the steps to where a door was bulging and splintering beneath the weapons of those beyond.

"Stand back, Moonglum."

Elric drew the crooning runesword, lifted it high and brought it against the door.

The door split and two oddly shaped skulls were split with it.

The remainder of the attackers fell back with cries of astonishment and horror as the white-faced reaver fell upon them, his huge sword drinking their souls and singing its strange, undulating song.

Down the stairs Elric pursued them. Into the hall where they bunched together and prepared to defend themselves from this demon with his hell-forged blade.

And Elric laughed.

And they shuddered.

And their weapons trembled in their hands.

"So you are the mighty Kelmain," Elric sneered. "No wonder you needed sorcery to aid you if you are so cowardly. Have you not heard, beyond World's Edge, of Elric Kinslayer?"

But the Kelmain plainly did not understand his speech, which was strange enough in itself, for he had spoken in the Common Tongue, known to all men.

These people had golden skins and eye-sockets that were almost square. Their faces, in all, seemed crudely carved from rock, all sharp angles and planes, and their armour was not rounded, but angular.

Elric bared his teeth in a smile and the Kelmain drew closer together.

Then he screamed with dreadful laughter and Moonglum stepped back and did not look at what took place.

The runesword swung. Heads and limbs were chopped away. Blood gouted. Souls were taken. The Kelmain's dead faces bore expressions showing that before the life was drawn from them they had known the truth of their appalling fate.

And Stormbringer drank again, for Stormbringer was a thirsty hellsword.

And Elric felt his deficient veins swell with even more energy than that which he had taken earlier from Theleb K'aarna's demon.

The hall shook with Elric's insane mirth and he strode over the piled corpses and he went through the open gateway to where the great host waited.

And he shouted a name:

"Theleb K'aarna, Theleb K'aarna!"

Moonglum ran after him, calling for him to stop, but Elric did not heed him. Elric strode on through the snow, his sword dripping a red trail behind him.

Under a cold sun, the Kelmain were riding for the castle called Kaneloon and Elric went to meet them.

At their head, on slender horses, rode the dark-faced sorcerer of Pan Tang, dressed in flowing robes, and beside him was the Prince of the Kelmain Host, Prince Umbda, in proud armour, bizarre plumes nodding on his helm, a triumphant smile on his strange, angular features.

Behind, the host dragged oddly-fashioned wargear which, for all its oddness, looked powerful—mightier than anything Lormyr could rally when the huge army fell upon her.

As the lone figure appeared and began to walk away from the walls of Castle Kaneloon Theleb K'aarna raised his hand and stopped the host's advance, reining in his own horse and laughing.

"Why, it is the jackal of Melniboné, by all the Gods of Chaos! He acknowledges his master at last and comes to deliver himself up to me!"

Elric came closer and Theleb K'aarna laughed on. "Here, Elric—kneel before me!"

Elric did not pause, seemed not to hear the Pan Tangian's words.

Prince Umbda's eyes were troubled and he said something in a strange tongue. Theleb K'aarna sniffed and replied in the same language.

And still the albino marched through the snow towards the huge host.

"By Chardros, Elric, stop!" cried Theleb K'aarna, his horse shifting nervously beneath him. "If you have come to bargain you are a fool. Kaneloon and her mistress must fall before Lormyr is ours—and Lormyr shall be ours, there's no doubting that!"

Then Eric did stop and he brought up his eyes to burn into those of the sorcerer and there was a still, cold smile upon his pale lips.

Theleb K'aarna tried to meet Elric's gaze but could not. His voice trembled when he next spoke.

"You cannot defeat the whole Kelmain Host!"

"I have no wish to, conjurer. Your life is all I desire."

The sorcerer's face twitched. "Well, you shall not have it! Hai, men of the Kelmain, take him!"

He wheeled his horse and rode into the protective ranks of his warriors, calling out his orders in their own tongue.

From the castle another figure burst, rushing to join Elric.

It was Moonglum of Elwher, a sword in either hand. Elric half-turned.

"Elric! We'll die together!"

"Stay back, Moonglum!"

Moonglum hesitated.

"Stay back, if you love me!"

Moonglum reluctantly retreated to the castle.

The Kelmain horsemen swept in, broad-bladed straight swords raised, instantly surrounding the albino.

They threatened him, hoping that he would lay down his sword and let himself be captured. But Elric smiled.

Stormbringer began to sing. Elric grasped the sword in both hands, bent his elbows then suddenly held the blade straight out before him.

He began to whirl like a Tarkeshite dancer, round and round, and it was as if the sword dragged him faster and faster while it gouged and gashed and decapitated the Kelmain horsemen.

For a moment they fell back, leaving their dead comrades heaped about the albino, but Prince Umbda, after a hurried conference with Theleb K'aarna, urged them upon Elric again.

And Elric swung his blade once more, but not so many of the Kelmain perished this time.

Armoured body fell against amoured body, blood mingled with brother's blood, horses dragged corpses away with them across the snow and Elric did not fall, yet something was happening to him.

Then it dawned upon his berserker brain that, for some reason, his blade was sated. The energy still pulsed in its metal, but it transferred nothing more to its master. And his own stolen energy was beginning to wane.

"Damn you, Stormbringer! Give me your power!"

Swords rained down upon him as he fought and slew and parried and thrust.

"More power!"

He was still stronger than normal and much stronger than any ordinary mortal, but some of the wild anger was leaving him and he felt almost puzzled as more Kelmain came at him.

He was beginning to waken from the blood-dream.

He shook his head and drew deep breaths. His back was aching.

"Give me their strength, Black Sword!"

He struck at legs and arms and chests and faces and he was covered from head to foot in the blood of his attackers.

But the dead now hampered him worse than the living, for their corpses were everywhere and he almost lost his footing more than once.

"What ails you, runesword? Do you refuse to help me? Will you not fight these things because, like you, they are of Chaos?"

No, it could not be that. All that had happened was that the sword desired no more vitality and therefore gave Elric none.

He fought on for another hour before his grip on the sword weakened and a rider, half-mad with terror, struck a blow at his head, failed to split it but stunned him so that he fell upon the bodies of the slain, tried to rise, then was struck again and lost consciousness.

CHAPTER EIGHT

A Great Host Screaming

"It was more than I hoped," murmured Theleb K'aarna in satisfaction, "but we have taken him alive!"

Elric opened his eyes and looked with hatred on the sorcerer who was stroking his black forked beard as if to comfort himself.

Elric could barely remember the events which had brought him here and placed him in the sorcerer's power. He remembered much blood, much laughter, much dying, but it was all fading, like the memory of a dream.

"Well, renegade, your foolishness was unbelievable. I thought you must have an army behind you. But doubtless it was your fear which unbalanced your poor brain. Still, I'll not speculate upon the cause of my own good fortune. There's many a bargain I can strike with the denizens of other planes, were I to offer them your soul. And your body I will keep for myself—to show Queen Yishana what I did to her lover before he died. . . ."

Elric laughed shortly and looked about him, ignoring Theleb K'aarna.

The Kelmain were awaiting orders. They had still not marched on Kaneloon. The sun was low in the sky. He saw the pile of corpses behind him. He saw the hatred and fear on the faces of the golden-skinned Host and he smiled again.

"I do not love Yishana," he said distantly, as if scarcely aware of Theleb K'aarna's presence. "It is your jealous heart that makes you think so. I left Yishana's

59

side to find you. It is never love that moves Elric of
Melniboné, sorcerer, but always hatred."

"I do not believe you," Theleb K'aarna tittered.
"When the whole South falls to me and my comrades,
then will I court Yishana and offer to make her Queen
of all the West as well as all the South. Our forces
united, we shall dominate the Earth!"

"You Pan Tangians were ever an insecure breed, forever planning conquest for its own sake, forever seeking
to destroy the equilibrium of the Young Kingdoms."

"One day," sneered Theleb K'aarna, "Pan Tang will
have an empire that will make the Bright Empire seem
a mere flickering ember in the fire of history. But it is
not for the glory of Pan Tang that I do this. . . ."

"It is for Yishana? By the gods, sorcerer, then I am
glad I'm motivated by hatred and not by love, for I do
not half the damage, it seems, done by those in love. . . ."

"I will lay the south at Yishana's feet and she may
use it as she pleases!"

"I am bored by this. What do you intend to do with
me?"

"First I will hurt your body. I will hurt it delicately
to begin with, building up the pain, until I have you in
the proper frame of mind. Then I will consort with the
Lords of the Higher Planes to find which will give me
most for your soul."

"And what of Kaneloon?"

"The Kelmain will deal with Kaneloon. One knife is
all that's needed now to slit Myshella's throat as she
sleeps."

"She is protected."

Theleb K'aarna's brow darkened. Then it cleared
and he laughed again.

"Aye, but the gate will fall soon enough and your
little redhaired friend will perish as Myshella perishes."

He ran his fingers through his oiled ringlets.

"I am allowing, at Prince Umbda's request, the Kelmain to rest a while before storming the castle. But
Kaneloon will be burning by nightfall."

Elric looked towards the castle across the trampled

snow. Plainly his runes had failed to counter Theleb
K'aarna's spell.,

"I would. . . ." He began to speak when he paused.

He had seen a flash of gold and silver among the
battlements and a thought without shape had entered
his head and made him hesitate.

"What?" Theleb K'aarna asked him harshly.

"Nothing. I merely wondered where my sword was."

The sorcerer shrugged. "Nowhere you can reach it,
reaver. We left it where you dropped it. The stinking
hellblade is no use to us. And none to you, now. . . ."

Elric wondered what would happen if he made a
direct appeal to the sword. He could not get to it himself, for Theleb K'aarna had bound him tightly with
ropes of silk, but he might *call* for it. . . .

He lifted himself to his feet.

"Would you seek to run away, White Wolf?" Theleb K'aarna watched him nervously.

Elric smiled again. "I wished for a better view of
the coming conquest of Kaneloon. Just that."

The sorcerer drew a curved knife.

Elric swayed, his eyes half-closed, and he began to
murmur a name beneath his breath.

Theleb K'aarna leapt forward and his arm encircled
Elric's head while the knife pricked into the albino's
throat. "Be silent, jackal!"

But Elric knew that he had no other means of helping
himself and, for all it was a desperate scheme, he murmured the words once more, praying that Theleb
K'aarna's lust for a slow revenge would make the
sorcerer hesitate before killing him.

Theleb K'aarna cursed, trying to prise Elric's mouth
open.

"The first thing I'll do is cut out that damned tongue
of yours!"

Elric bit the hand and tasted the sorcerer's blood.
He spat it out.

Theleb K'aarna screamed. "By Chardros, if I did
not wish to see you die over the months, I would . . ."

And then a sound came from the Kelmain.

It was a moan of surprise and it issued from every throat.

Theleb K'aarna turned and the breath hissed from between his clenched teeth.

Through the murky dusk a black shape moved. It was the sword, Stormbringer.

Elric had called it.

Now he cried aloud:

"Stormbringer! Stormbringer! To me!"

Theleb K'aarna flung Elric in the path of the sword and rushed into the security of the gathered ranks of Kelmain warriors.

"Stormbringer!"

The black sword hovered in the air near Elric.

Another shout went up from the Kelmain. A shape had left the battlements of Castle Kaneloon.

Theleb K'aarna shouted in hysteria. "Prince Umbda! Prepare your men for the attack! I sense danger to us!"

Umbda could not understand the sorcerer's words and Theleb K'aarna was forced to translate them.

"Do not let the sword reach him!" cried the sorcerer. Once more he shouted in the language of the Kelmain and several warriors ran forward to grasp the rune-sword before it could reach its albino master.

But the sword struck rapidly and the Kelmain died and none dared approach it after that.

Slowly Stormbringer moved towards Elric.

"Ah, Elric," cried Theleb K'aarna, "if you escape me this day, I swear that I shall find you."

"And if you escape me," Elric shouted back, "I will find you, Theleb K'aarna. Be sure of that."

The shape that had left Castle Kaneloon had feathers of silver and gold. It flew high above the Host and hovered for a moment before moving to the outer edges of the gathering. Elric could not see it clearly, but he knew what it was. That was why he had summoned the sword, for he had an idea that Moonglum rode the giant bird of metal and that the Elwherian would try to rescue him.

"Do not let it land! It comes to save the albino!" screamed Theleb K'aarna.

But the Kelmain Host did not understand him. Under Prince Umbda's commands they were preparing themselves for the attack upon the castle.

Theleb K'aarna repeated his orders in their own tongue, but it was plain they were beginning not to trust him and could not see the need to bother themselves with one man and a strange bird of metal. It could not stop their engines of war. Neither could the man.

"Stormbringer," whispered Elric as the sword sliced through his bonds and gently settled in his hand. Elric was free, but the Kelmain, though not placing the same importance upon him as did Theleb K'aarna, showed that they were not prepared to let him escape now that the blade was in his grasp and not moving of its own volition.

Prince Umbda shouted something.

A huge mass of warriors rushed at Elric at once and he made no effort to take the attack to them this time for he was interested in fighting a defensive strategy until Moonglum could descend on the bird and help him.

But the bird was even further away. It appeared to be circling the outer perimeters of the host and showed no interest in his plight at all.

Had he been deceived?

He parried a dozen thrusts, letting the Kelmain warriors crowd in upon each other and thus hamper themselves. The bird of gold and silver was almost out of sight now.

And Theleb K'aarna—where was he?

Elric tried to find him, but the sorcerer was doubtless somewhere in the centre of the Kelmain ranks by now.

Elric killed a golden-skinned warrior, slitting his throat with the point of the runesword. More strength began to flow into him again. He killed another Kelmain with an overarm movement which split the man's shoulder. But nothing could be gained from this fight if Moonglum was not coming on the bird of silver and gold.

The bird seemed to change course and come back towards Kaneloon. Was it merely waiting for instructions from its sleeping mistress? Or was it refusing to obey Moonglum's commands?

Elric backed through the muddy, bloody snow so that the pile of corpses now lay behind him. He fought on, but with very little hope.

The bird went past, far to his right.

Elric thought ironically that he had completely mistaken the significance of the bird's leaving the castle battlements and by mistiming his decision had merely brought his death closer—perhaps Myshella's and Moonglum's deaths closer, too.

Kaneloon was doomed. Myshella was doomed. Lormyr and perhaps the whole of the Young Kingdoms were doomed.

And he was doomed.

It was then that a shadow passed across the battling men and the Kelmain screamed and fell back as a great din rent the air.

Elric looked up in relief, hearing the sound of the metal bird's clashing wings. He looked for Moonglum in the saddle and saw instead the tense face of Myshella herself, her hair blowing around her face as it was disturbed by the beating wings.

"Quickly, Lord Elric, before they close in again."

Elric sheathed the runesword and leapt towards the saddle, swinging himself behind the Sorceress of Kaneloon. Then they rose into the air again, while arrows hurtled around their heads and bounced off the bird's metal feathers.

"One more circuit of the Host and then we return to the castle," she said. "Your rune and the Nanorion worked to defeat Theleb K'aarna's enchantment, but they took longer than either of us would have liked. See, already Prince Umbda is ordering his men to mount and ride to Castle Kaneloon. And Kaneloon has only Moonglum to defend her now."

"Why this circuit of Umbda's army?"

"You will see. At least, I hope you will see, my lord."

She began to sing a song. It was a strange, disturbing chant in a language not dissimilar to the Melnibonéan High Speech, yet different enough for Elric to understand only a few words, for it was oddly accented.

Around the camp they flew. Elric saw the Kelmain form their ranks into battle order. Doubtless Umbda and Theleb K'aarna had by now decided on the best mode of attack.

Then back to the castle beat the great bird, settling on the battlements and allowing Elric and Myshella to dismount. Moonglum, his features taut, came running to meet them.

They went to look at the Kelmain.

And they saw that the Kelmain were on the move.

"What did you do to—" began Elric, but Myshella raised her hand.

"Perhaps I did nothing. Perhaps the sorcery will not work."

"What was it you . . . ?"

"I scattered the contents of the purse you brought. I scattered it around their whole army. Watch. . . ."

"And if the spell has not worked—" Moonglum murmured. He paused, straining his eyes through the gloom. "What is that?"

Myshella's satisfied tone was almost ghoulish as she said: "It is the Noose of Flesh."

Something was growing out of the snow. Something pink that quivered. Something huge. A great mass that arose on all sides of the Kelmain and made their horses rear up and snort.

And it made the Kelmain shriek.

The stuff was like flesh and it had grown so high that the whole Kelmain Host was obscured from sight. There were noises as they tried to train their battle-engines upon the stuff and blast their way through.

There were shouts. But not a single horseman broke out of the Noose of Flesh.

Then the substance began to fold in over the Kelmain and Elric heard a sound such as none he had heard before.

It was a voice.

A voice of a hundred thousand men all facing an identical terror, all dying an identical death.

It was a moan of desperation, of hopelessness, of fear.

But it was a moan so loud that it shook the walls of Castle Kaneloon.

"It is no death for a warrior," murmured Moonglum, turning away.

"But it was the only weapon we had," said Myshella. "I have possessed it for a good many years but never before did I feel the need to use it."

"Of them all, only Theleb K'aarna deserved that death," said Elric.

Night fell and the Noose of Flesh tightened around the Kelmain Host, crushing all but a few horses which had run free as the sorcery began to work.

It crushed Prince Umbda, who spoke no language known in the Young Kingdoms, who spoke no language known to the ancients, who had come to conquer from beyond the World's Edge.

It crushed Theleb K'aarna, who had sought, for the sake of his love for a wanton Queen, to conquer the world with the aid of Chaos.

It crushed all the warriors of that near-human race, the Kelmain. And it crushed all who could have told the watchers what the Kelmain had been or from where they had originated.

Then it absorbed them. Then it flickered and dissolved and was dust again.

No piece of flesh—man's nor beast's—remained. But over the snow was scattered clothing, arms, armour, siege engines, riding accoutrements, coins, belt-buckles, for as far as the eye could see.

Myshella nodded to herself. "That was the Noose of

Flesh," she said. "I thank you for bringing it to me, Elric. I thank you, also, for finding the stone which revived me. I thank you for saving Lormyr."

"Aye," said Elric. "Thank me." There was a weariness on him now. He turned away, shivering.

Snow had begun to fall again.

"Thank me for nothing, Lady Myshella. What I did was to satisfy my own dark urges, to sate my thirst for vengeance. I have destroyed Theleb K'aarna. The rest was incidental. I care nought for Lormyr, the Young Kingdoms, or any of your causes. . . ."

Moonglum saw that Myshella had a sceptical look in her eyes and she smiled slightly.

Elric entered the castle and began to descend the steps to the hall.

"Wait," Myshella said. "This castle is magical. It reflects the desires of any who enter it—should I wish it."

Elric rubbed at his eyes. "Then plainly we have no desires. Mine are satisfied now that Theleb K'aarna is destroyed. I would leave this place now, my lady."

"You have none?" said she.

He looked at her directly. He frowned. "Regret breeds weakness. Regret achieves nothing. Regret is like a disease which attacks the internal organs and at last destroys. . . ."

"And you have no desires?"

He hesitated. "I understand you. Your own appearance, I'll admit. . . ." He shrugged. "But are you—?"

She spread her hands. "Do not ask too many questions of me." She made another gesture. "Now. See. This castle becomes what you most desire. And in it, the things you most desire!"

And Elric looked about him, his eyes widening, and he began to scream.

He fell to his knees in terror. He turned pleadingly to her.

"No, Myshella! No. I do not desire this!"

Hastily she made yet another sign.

Moonglum helped his friend to his feet. "What was it? What did you see?"

Elric straightened his back and rested his hand on his sword and said grimly and quietly to Myshella:

"Lady, I would kill you for that if I did not understand you sought only to please me."

He studied the ground for a moment before continuing:

"Know this. Elric cannot have what he desires most. What he desires does not exist. What he desires is dead. All Elric has is sorrow, guilt, malice, hatred. This is all he deserves and all he will ever desire."

She put her hands to her own face and walked back to the room where he had first seen her. Elric followed.

Moonglum started after them but then he stopped and remained where he stood.

He watched them enter the room and saw the door close.

He walked back on to the battlements and stared into the darkness. He saw wings of silver and gold flashing in the moonlight and they became smaller and smaller until they had vanished.

He sighed. It was cold.

He went back into the castle and settled himself with his back against a pillar, preparing to sleep.

But a little while later he heard laughter come from the room in the highest tower.

And the laughter sent him running through the passages, through the great hall where the fire had died, out of the door, into the night to seek the stables where he could feel more secure.

But he could not sleep that night, for the distant laughter still pursued him.

And the laughter continued until morning.

BOOK TWO

To Snare the Pale Prince

". . . but it was in Nadsokor, City of Beggars, that Elric found an old friend and learned something concerning an old enemy . . ."

—*The Chronicle of the Black Sword*

CHAPTER ONE

The Beggar Court

Nadsokor, city of Beggars, was infamous throughout the Young Kingdoms. Lying near the shores of that ferocious river, the Varkalk, and not too far from the Kingdom of Org in which blossomed the frightful Forest of Troos, and exuding a stink which seemed thick enough ten miles distant, Nadsokor was plagued by few visitors.

From this unlovely place sallied out her citizens to beg their way about the world and steal what they could and bring it back to Nadsokor where half of their profits were handed over to their king in return for his protection.

Their king had ruled for many years. He was called Urish the Seven-fingered, for he had but four fingers on his right hand and three upon his left. Veins had burst all over his once handsome face and filthy, infested hair framed that seedy countenance upon which age and grime had traced a thousand lines. From out of all this ruin peered two bright, pale eyes.

As the symbol of his power Urish had a great cleaver called Hackmeat which was forever at his side. His throne was of crudely carved black oak, studded with bits of raw gold, bones and semi-precious gems. Beneath this throne was Urish's Hoard—a chest of treasure which he let none but himself look upon.

For the best part of every day Urish would lounge on his throne, presiding over a gloomy, festering hall throned with his Court: a rabble of rascals too foul in appearance and disposition to be tolerated anywhere but here.

For heat and light there burned permanently braziers of garbage which gave out oily smoke and a stink which dominated all the other stinks in the hall.

And now there was a visitor at Urish's Court.

He stood before the dais on which the throne was mounted and from time to time he raised a heavily scented kerchief to his red, full lips.

His face, which was normally dark in complexion, was somewhat grey and his eyes had something of a haunted, tortured look in them as they glanced from begrimed beggar to pile of rubbish to guttering brazier. Dressed in the loose brocade robes of the folk of Pan Tang, the visitor had black eyes, a great hooked nose, blue-black ringlets and a curling beard. Kerchief to mouth, he bowed low when he reached Urish's throne.

As always, greed, weakness and malice mingled to form King Urish's expression as he regarded the stranger whom one of his courtiers had but lately announced.

Urish had recognised the name and he believed he could guess the Pan Tangian's business here.

"I heard you were dead, Theleb K'aarna—killed beyond Lormyr, near World's Edge." Urish grinned to display the black crags which were the rotting remains of his teeth.

Theleb K'aarna removed the kerchief from his lips and his voice was strangled at first, gaining strength as he remembered the wrongs recently done him. "My magic is not so weak I cannot escape a spell such as was woven that day. I conjured myself below the ground while Myshella's Noose of Flesh engulfed the Kelmain Host."

Urish's disgusting grin widened.

"You crept into a hole, is that it?"

The sorcerer's eyes burned fiercely. "I'll not dispute the strength of my powers with—"

He broke off and drew a deep breath which he at once regretted. He stared warily around him at the Beggar Court, all manged and maimed, which had deposited itself about the filthy hall, mocking him. The beggars of Nadsokor knew the power of poverty and disease—knew how it terrified those who were not used to it. And thus their very squalor was their safeguard against intruders.

A repulsive cough which might have been a laugh now seized King Urish. "And was it your magic that brought you here?" As his whole body shook his bloodshot eyes continued, beadily, to regard the sorcerer.

"I have travelled across the seas and all across Vilmir to be here," Theleb K'aarna said, "because I had heard there was one you hated above all others. . . ."

"And we hate *all* others—all who are not beggars," Urish reminded him. The king chuckled and the chuckle became, once more, a throaty, convulsive cough.

"But you hate Elric of Melniboné most."

"Aye. It would be fair to say that. Before he won fame as the Kinslayer, the traitor of Imrryr, he came to Nadsokor to deceive us, disguised as a leper who had begged his way from the Eastlands beyond Karlaak. He tricked me disgracefully and stole something from my Hoard. And my Hoard is sacred—I will not let another even glimpse it!"

"I heard he stole a scroll from you," Theleb K'aarna said. "A spell which had once belonged to his cousin Yyrkoon. Yyrkoon wished to be rid of Elric and let him believe that the spell would release the Princess Cymoril from her sorcerous slumber. . . ."

"Aye. Yyrkoon had given the scroll to one of our citizens when he went a-begging to the gates of Imrryr. He then told Elric what he had done. Elric disguised himself and came here. With the aid of sorcery he gained access to my Hoard—my sacred Hoard—and plucked the scroll from it. . . ."

Theleb K'aarna looked sideways at the Beggar King. "Some would say that it was not Elric's fault—that Yyrkoon was to blame. He deceived you both. The spell did not awaken Cymoril, did it?"

"No. But we have a Law in Nadsokor. . . ." Urish raised the great cleaver Hackmeat and displayed its ragged, rusty blade. For all its battered appearance, it was a fearsome weapon. "That Law says that any man who looks upon the sacred Hoard of King Urish must die and die most horribly—at the hands of the Burning God!"

"And none of your wandering citizens have yet managed to take this vengeance?"

"I must pass the sentence personally upon him before he dies. He must come again to Nadsokor, for it is only here that he may be acquainted with his doom."

Theleb K'aarna said: "I have no love for Elric."

Urish once more voiced the sound that was half laugh, half wheezing cough. "Aye—I have heard he has chased you all across the Young Kingdoms, that you have brought more and more powerful sorceries against him, yet every time he has defeated you."

Theleb K'aarna frowned. "Have a care, King Urish. I have had bad luck, yet I am still one of Pan Tang's greatest sorcerers."

"But you spend your powers freely and claim much from the Lords of Chaos. One day they will be tired of helping you and find another to do their work." King Urish closed soiled lips over black teeth. His pale eyes did not blink as he studied Theleb K'aarna.

There were stirrings in the hall, the Beggar Court moved in closer: the click of a crutch, the scrape of a staff, the shuffle of misshapen feet. Even the oily smoke from the braziers seemed to menace him as it drifted reluctantly into the darkness of the roof.

King Urish put one hand upon Hackmeat and the other upon his chin. Broken nails caressed stubble. From somewhere behind Theleb K'aarna a beggar woman let forth an obscene noise and then giggled.

Almost as if to comfort himself the sorcerer placed the scented kerchief firmly over his mouth and nostrils. He began to draw himself up, prepared to deal with an attack if it came.

"But you still have your powers now, I take it," said Urish suddenly, breaking the tension. "Or you would not be here."

"My powers increase. . . ."

"For the moment, perhaps."

"My powers . . ."

"I take it you come with a scheme which you hope will result in Elric's destruction," continued Urish easily. The beggars relaxed. Only Theleb K'aarna now showed any signs of discomfort. Urish's bright, blood-shot eyes were sardonic. "And you desire our help because you know we hate the white-faced reaver of Melniboné."

Theleb K'aarna nodded. "Would you hear the details of my plan?"

Urish shrugged. "Why not? At least they may be entertaining."

Unhappily, Theleb K'aarna looked about him at the corrupt and tittering crew. He wished he knew a spell which would disperse the stink.

He took a deep breath through his kerchief and then began to speak. . . .

CHAPTER TWO

The Stolen Ring

On the other side of the tavern the young dandy pretended to order another skin of wine while actually taking a sly look towards the corner where Elric sat.

Then the dandy leaned towards his compatriots—merchants and young nobles of several nations—and continued his murmured discourse.

The subject of that discourse, Elric knew, was Elric. Normally he was disdainful of such behaviour, but he was weary and he was impatient for Moonglum to return. He was almost tempted to order the young dandy to desist, if only to pass the time.

Elric was beginning to regret his decision to visit Old Hrolmar.

This rich city was a great meeting place for all the imaginative people of the Young Kingdoms. To it came explorers, adventurers, mercenaries, craftsmen, merchants, painters and poets for, under the rule of the famous Duke Avan Astran, this Vilmirian city state was undergoing a transformation in its character.

Duke Avan was himself a man who had explored most of the world and had brought back great wealth and knowledge to Old Hrolmar. Its riches and its intellectual life attracted more riches, more intellectuals and so Old Hrolmar flourished.

But where riches are and where intellectuals are, then gossip also flourishes, for if there is any breed of man who gossips more than the merchant or the sailor then it is the poet and the painter. And, naturally enough, there was much gossip concerning the doom-driven albino, Elric, already a hero of several ballads by poets not over-talented.

Elric had allowed himself to be brought to the city because Moonglum had said it was the best place to find an income. Elric's carelessness with their wealth had made near-paupers of them, not for the first time, and they were in need of provisions and fresh steeds.

Elric had been for skirting Old Hrolmar and riding on towards Tanelorn, where they had decided to go, but Moonglum had argued reasonably that they would need better horses and more food and equipment for the long ride across the Vilmirian and Ilmioran plains to the edge of the Sighing Desert, where mysterious Tanelorn was situated. So Elric had at last agreed, though, after his encounter with Myshella and his witnessing of the destruction of the Noose of Flesh, he had become weary and craved for the peace which Tanelorn offered.

What made things worse was that this tavern was rather too well-lit and catering too much to the better end of the trade for Elric's taste. He would have preferred a lowlier sort of inn which would have been cheaper and where men were used to holding back their questions and their gossip. But Moonglum had thought it wise to spend the last of their wealth on a good inn, in case they should need to entertain someone. . . .

Elric left the business of raising treasure to Moonglum. Doubtless he intended to get it by thievery or trickery, but Elric did not care.

He sighed and suffered the sidelong looks of the other guests and tried not to overhear the young dandy. He sipped his cup of wine and picked at the flesh of the cold fowl Moonglum had ordered before he went off. He drew his head into the high collar of his black cloak, but succeeded only in emphasising the bone-white pallor of his face and the milky whiteness of his long hair. He looked around him at the silks and furs and tapestries swirling about the tavern as their owners moved from table to table and he longed with all his heart to be on his way to Tanelorn, where men spoke little because they had experienced so much.

". . . killed mother and father, too—and the mother's lover, it is said. . . ."

". . . and they say he lies with corpses for preference. . . ."

". . . and because of that the Lords of the Higher Worlds cursed him with the face of a corpse. . . ."

"Incest, was it not? I got it from one who sailed with him that . . ."

". . . and his mother had congress with Arioch himself, thus producing . . ."

". . . shortly before he betrayed his own people to Smiorgan and the rest!"

"He looks a gloomy fellow, right enough. Not one to enjoy a jest. . . ."

Laughter.

Elric made himself relax in his chair and swallow more wine. But the gossip went on.

"They say also that he is an imposter. That the real Elric died at Imrryr. . . ."

"A true prince of Melniboné would dress in more lavish style. And he would . . ."

More laughter.

Elric stood up, pushing back his cloak so that the great black broadsword at his hip was fully displayed. Most people in Old Hrolmar had heard of the runesword Stormbringer and its terrible power.

Elric crossed to the table where the young dandy sat.

"I pray you, gentlemen, to improve your sport! You can do much better now—for here is one who would offer you proof of certain things of which you speak. What of his penchant for vampirism of a particular sort? I did not hear you touch upon that in your conversation."

The young dandy cleared his throat and made a nervous little flirt of his shoulder.

"Well?" Elric feigned an innocent expression. "Cannot I be of assistance?"

The gossips had become dumb, pretending to be absorbed in their eating and drinking.

Elric smiled a smile which set their hands to shaking.

"I desire only to know what you wish to hear, gentlemen. Then I will demonstrate that I am truly the one you have called Elric Kinslayer."

The merchants and the nobles gathered their rich robes about them and, avoiding his eye, got up. The young dandy minced towards the exit—a parody of bravado.

But now Elric stood laughing in the doorway, his hand on the hilt of Stormbringer. "Will you not join me as my guests, gentlemen? Think how you could tell your friends of the meeting. . . ."

"Gods, how boorish!" lisped the young dandy and then shivered.

"Sir, we meant no harm . . ." thickly said a fat Shazarian herb trader.

"We spoke of another." A young noble with only the hint of a chin, but with an emphatic moustache, offered a feeble, placatory grin.

"We said how much we admired you . . ." stuttered a Vilmirian knight whose eyes appeared but recently to have crossed and whose face was now almost as pale as Elric's.

A merchant in the dark brocades of Tarkesh licked his red lips and attempted to conduct himself with more dignity than his friends. "Sir, Old Hrolmar is a civilised city. Gentlemen do not brawl amongst themselves here. . . ."

"But like peasant women prefer to gossip," said Elric.

"Yes," said the youth with the abundance of moustache. "Ah—no. . . ."

The dandy arranged his cloak about him and glowered at the floor.

Elric stepped aside. Uncertainly the Tarkeshite merchant moved forward and then ran for the darkness of the street, his companions tumbling behind him. Elric heard their footsteps running on the cobbles and he began to laugh. At the sound of his laugh the footfalls became a scamper and the party had soon reached the quayside where the water gleamed, turned a corner and disappeared.

Elric smiled and looked up beyond Old Hrolmar's baroque skyline at the stars. Now there were more footsteps coming from the other end of the street. He turned and saw the newcomers step into a pool of light thrown from the window of a nearby office.

It was Moonglum. The stocky Eastlander was returning in the company of two women who were scantily dressed and heavily painted and who were without doubt Vilmirian whores from the other side of city. Moonglum had an arm about each waist and he was singing some obscure but evidently disgraceful ballad, pausing frequently to have one of the laughing girls pour wine down his throat. Both the whores had large stone flasks in their free hands and they were matching Moonglum drink for drink.

As Moonglum stepped unsteadily nearer he recognised Elric and hailed him, winking. "You see I have not forgotten you, Prince of Melniboné. One of these beauties is for you!"

Elric made an exaggerated bow. "You are very good to me. But I thought you planned to find some gold for us. Was that not the reason for coming to Old Hrolmar?"

"Aye!" Moonglum kissed the cheeks of the girls. They snorted with laughter. "Indeed! Gold it is—or something as good as gold. I have rescued these young ladies from a cruel whoremaster on the other side of town. I have promised to sell them to a kinder master and they are grateful to me!"

"You stole these slaves?"

"If you wish to say so—I 'stole' them. Aye, then, 'steal' I did. I stole in with my steel and I released them from a life of degradation. A humanitarian deed. Their miserable life is no more! They may look forward to . . ."

"Their miserable lives will be no more—as, indeed,

will be ours when the whoremaster discovers the crime and alerts the watch. How found you these ladies?"

"They found me! I had made my swords available to an old merchant, a stranger to the city. I was to escort him about the murkier regions of Old Hrolmar in return for a good purse of gold (better, I think, than he expected to give me). While he whored above, as he could, I had a drink or two below in the public rooms. These two beauties look a liking to me and told me of their unhappiness. It was enough. I rescued them."

"A cunning plan," Elric said sardonically.

" 'Twas theirs! They have brains as well as—"

"I'll help you carry them back to their master before the city guards descend upon us."

"But Elric!"

"But first . . ." Elric seized his friend and threw him over his shoulder, staggering with him to the quay at the end of the street, taking a good hold on his collar and lowering him suddenly into the reeking water. Then he hauled him up and stood him down. Moonglum shivered and looked sadly at Elric.

"I am prone to colds, as you know."

"And prone to drunken plans, too! We are not liked here, Moonglum. The watch needs only one excuse to set upon us. At best we should have to flee the city before our business was done. At worst we shall be disarmed, imprisoned, perhaps slain."

They began to walk back to where the two girls still stood. One of the girls ran forward and knelt to take Elric's hand and press her lips against his thigh. "Master, I have a message. . . ."

Elric bent to raise her to her feet.

She screamed. Her painted eyes widened. He stared at her in astonishment and then, following her gaze, turned and saw the pack of bravos who had stolen round the corner and were now rushing at himself and Moonglum. Behind the bravos Elric thought he saw the young dandy he had earlier chased from the tavern. The dandy wished for revenge. Poignards glit-

tered in the darkness and their owners wore the black
hoods of professional assassins. There were at least a
dozen of them. The young dandy must therefore be
extremely rich, for assassins were expensive in Old
Hrolmar.

Moonglum had already drawn both his swords and
was engaging the leader. Elric pushed the frightened
girl behind him and put his hand to Stormbringer's
pommel. Almost at its own volition the huge runesword
sprang from its scabbard and black light poured from
its blade as it began to hum its own strange battle-cry.

He heard one of the assassins gasp "Elric!" and
guessed that the dandy had not made it plain whom
they were to slay. He blocked the thrust of the slim
longsword, turned it and chopped with a kind of deli-
cacy at the owner's wrist. Wrist and sword flew into
the shadows and the owner staggered back screaming.

More swords now and more cold eyes glittering from
the black hoods. Stormbringer sang its peculiar song—
half-lament, half-victory shout. Elric's own face was
alive with battle-lust and his crimson eyes blazed from
his bone-white face as he swung this way and that.

Shouts, curses, the screams of women and the groans
of men, steel striking steel, boots on cobbles, the sounds
of swords in flesh, of blades scraping bone. A confusion
through which Elric fought, his broadsword clapped
in both pale hands. He had lost sight of Moonglum and
prayed that the Eastlander still stood. From time to time
he glimpsed one of the girls and wondered why she had
not run for safety.

Now the corpses of several hooded assassins lay upon
the cobbles and the remainder were beginning to falter
as Elric pressed them. They knew the power of his
sword and what it did to those it struck. They had seen
their comrades' faces as their souls were drawn from
them by the hellblade. With every death Elric seemed
to grow stronger and the black radiance from the blade
seemed to burn fiercer. And now the albino was laughing.

His laughter rang over the rooftops of Old Hrolmar

and those who were abed covered their ears, believing themselves in the grip of nightmares.

"Come, friends, my blade still hungers!"

An assassin made to stand his ground and Elric swept the Black Sword up. The man raised his blade to protect his head and Elric brought the Black Sword down. It sheared through the steel and cut down through the hood, through the neck, through the breastbone. It clove the assassin completely in two and it stayed in the flesh, feasting, drawing out the last traces of the man's dark soul. And then the rest were running.

Elric drew a deep breath, avoided looking at the man his sword had slain last, sheathed the blade and turned to look for Moonglum.

It was then that the blow came on the back of his neck. He felt nausea rise in him and tried to shake it off. He felt a prick in his wrist and through the haze he saw a figure he thought at first was Moonglum. But it was another—perhaps a woman. She was tugging at his left hand. Where did she want him to go?

His knees became weak and he fell to the cobbles. He tried to call out, but failed. The woman was still tugging at his hand as if she sought to take him to safety. But he could not follow her. He fell on his shoulder, then on his back, glimpsed a swimming sky . . .

. . . and then the dawn was rising over the crazy spires of Old Hrolmar and he realised that several hours had passed since he had fought the assassins.

Moonglum's face appeared. It was full of concern.

"Moonglum?"

"Thank Elwher's gentle gods! I thought you slain by that poisoned blade."

Elric's head was clearing rapidly now. He rose to a sitting position. "The attacker came from behind. How . . . ?"

Moonglum looked embarrassed. "I fear those girls were not all they seemed."

Elric remembered the woman tugging at his left hand

and he stretched out his fingers. "Moonglum! The Ring of Kings is gone from my hand! The Actorios has been stolen!"

The Ring of Kings had been worn by Elric's forefathers for centuries. It had been the symbol of their power, the source of much of their supernatural strength.

Moonglum's face clouded. "I thought I stole the girls. But they were thieves. They planned to rob us. An old trick."

"There's more to it, Moonglum. They stole nothing else. Just the Ring of Kings. There's still a little gold left in my purse." He jingled his belt pouch, climbing to his feet.

Moonglum jerked his thumb at the street's far wall. There lay one of the girls, her finery all smeared with mud and blood.

"She got in the way of one of the assassins as we fought. She's been dying all night—mumbling your name. I had not told it to her. Therefore I fear you're right. They were sent to steal that ring from you. I was duped by them."

Elric walked rapidly to where the girl lay and he kneeled down beside her. Gently he touched her cheek. She opened her lids and stared at him from glazed eyes. Her lips formed his name.

"Why did you plan to rob me?" Elric asked. "Who is your master?"

"Urish . . ." she said in a voice that was a breeze passing through the grass. "Steal ring . . . take it to Nadsokor. . . ."

Moonglum now stood on the other side of the dying girl. He had found one of the wine flasks and he bent to give her a drink. She tried to sip the wine but failed. It ran down her little chin, down her slim neck and on to her wounded breast.

"You are one of the beggars of Nadsokor?" Moonglum said.

Faintly, she nodded.

"Urish has always been my enemy," Elric told him.

"I once recovered some property from him and he has never forgiven me. Perhaps he sought the Actorios ring in payment." He looked down at the girl. "Your companion—has she returned to Nadsokor?"

Again the girl seemed to nod. Then all intelligence left the eyes, the lids closed and she ceased to breathe.

Elric got up. He was frowning, rubbing at the hand on which the Ring of Kings had been.

"Let him keep the ring, then," said Moonglum hopefully. "He will be satisfied."

Elric shook his head.

Moonglum cleared his throat. "A caravan is leaving Jadmar in a week. It is commanded by Rackhir of Tanelorn and has been purchasing provisions for the city. If we took a ship round the coast we could soon be in Jadmar, join Rackhir's caravan and be on our way to Tanelorn in good company. As you know, it's rare for anyone of Tanelorn to make such a journey. We are lucky, for . . ."

"No," said Elric in a low voice. "We must forget Tanelorn for the moment, Moonglum, The Ring of Kings is my link with my fathers. More—it aids my conjurings and has saved our lives more than once. We ride for Nadsokor now. I must try to reach the girl before she gets to the City of Beggars. Failing that, I must enter the city and recover my ring."

Moonglum shuddered. "It would be more foolish than any plan of mine, Elric. Urish would destroy us."

"None the less, to Nadsokor I must go."

Moonglum bent and began systematically to strip the girl's corpse of its jewellery. "We'll need every penny we can raise if we're to buy decent horses for our journey," he explained.

CHAPTER THREE

The Cold Ghouls

Framed against the scarlet sunset, Nadsokor looked from this distance more like a badly kept graveyard than a city. Towers tottered, houses were half-collapsed, the walls were broken.

Elric and Moonglum came up the peak of the hill on their fast Shazarian horses (which had cost them all they had) and saw it. Worse—they smelled it. A thousand stinks issued from the festering city and both men gagged, turning their horses back down the hill to the valley.

"We'll camp here for a short while—until nightfall," Elric said. "Then we'll enter Nadsokor."

"Elric, I am not sure I could bear the stench. Whatever our disguise, our disgust would reveal us for strangers."

Elric smiled and reached into his pouch. He took out two small tablets and handed one to Moonglum.

The Eastlander regarded the thing suspiciously. "What's this?"

"A potion. I used it once before when I came to Nadsokor. It will kill your sense of smell completely—unfortunately your sense of taste as well. . . ."

Moonglum laughed. "I did not plan to eat a gourmet meal while in the City of Beggars!" He swallowed the pill and Elric did likewise.

Almost instantly Moonglum remarked that the stink of the city was subsiding. Later, as they chewed the stale bread which was all that was left of their provisions, he said:

"I can taste nothing. The potion works."

Elric nodded. He was frowning, looking up the hill in the direction of the city as the night fell.

Moonglum took out his swords and began to hone them with the small stone he carried for the purpose. As he honed, he watched Elric's face, trying to see if he could guess Elric's thoughts.

At last the albino spoke. "We'll need to leave the horses here, of course, for most beggars disdain their use."

"They are proud in their perversity," Moonglum murmured.

"Aye. We'll need those rags we brought."

"Our swords will be noticed. . . ."

"Not if we wear the loose robes over all. It will mean we'll walk stiff-legged, but that's not so strange in a beggar."

Reluctantly Moonglum got the bundles of rags from the saddle-panniers.

So it was that a filthy pair, one stooped and limping, one short but with a twisted arm, crept through the debris which was ankle deep around the whole city of Nadsokor. They made for one of the many gaps in the wall.

Nadsokor had been abandoned some centuries before by a people fleeing from the ravages of a particularly virulent pox which had struck down most of their number. Not long afterwards the first of the beggars had occupied it. Nothing had been done to preserve the city's defences and now the muck around the perimeters was as effective a protection as any wall.

No one saw the two figures as they climbed over the messy rubble and entered the dark, festering streets of the City of Beggars. Huge rats raised themselves on their hind legs and watched them as they made their way to what had once been Nadsokor's senate building and which was now Urish's palace. Scrawny dogs with garbage dangling in their jaws warily slunk back into the shadows. Once a little column of blind men, each man with his right hand on the shoulder of the man in front, tapped their way through the night, pass-

ing directly across the street Elric and Moonglum were
in. From some of the tumble-down buildings came
cacklings and titterings as the maimed caroused with
the crippled and the degenerate and corrupted coupled
with their crones. As the disguised pair neared what
had been Nadsokor's forum there came a scream from
one shattered doorway and a young girl, barely over
puberty, dashed out pursued by a monstrously fat beggar who propelled himself with astounding speed on
his crutches, the livid stumps of his legs, which termi-
nated at the knee, making the motions of running.
Moonglum tensed, but Elric held him back as the fat
cripple bore down his prey, abandoned his crutches
which rattled on the broken pavement, and flung himself on the child.

Moonglum tried to free himself from Elric's grasp
but the albino whispered: "Let it happen. Those who
are whole either in mind, body or spirit cannot be
tolerated in Nadsokor."

There were tears in Moonglum's eyes as he looked
at his friend. "Your cynicism is as disgusting as anything they do!"

"I do not doubt it. But we are here for one purpose
—to recover the stolen Ring of Kings. That, and nought
else, is what we shall do."

"What matters that when . ... ?"

But Elric was continuing on his way to the forum
and after hesitating for a moment Moonglum followed
him.

Now they stood on the far side of the square looking
at Urish's palace. Some of its columns had fallen, but
on this building alone had there been some attempt at
restoration and decoration. The archway of the main
entrance was painted with crude representations of the
Arts of Begging and Extortion. An example of the
coinage of all the nations of the Young Kingdoms had
been imbedded in the wooden door and above it had
been nailed, perhaps ironically, a pair of wooden
crutches, crossed as swords might be crossed, indicat-
ing that the weapons of the beggar were his power to

horrify and disgust those luckier or better endowed than himself.

Elric stared through the murk at the building and he had a calculating frown on his face.

"There are no guards," he said to Moonglum.

"Why should there be? What have they to guard?"

"There were guards last time I came to Nadsokor. Urish protects his hoard most assiduously. It is not outsiders he fears but his own despicable rabble."

"Perhaps he no longer fears them."

Elric smiled. "A creature like King Urish fears everything. We had best be wary when we enter the hall. Have your swords ready to draw at any hint that we have been lured into a trap."

"Surely Urish would not suspect we'd know where the girl came from?"

"Aye, it seemed good chance that one of them told us, but none the less we must make allowances for Urish's cunning."

"He would not willingly bring you here—not with the Black Sword at your side."

"Perhaps. . . ."

They began to walk across the forum. It was very still, very dark. From far away came the occasional shout, a laugh or an obscene, indefinable sound.

Now they were at the door, standing beneath the crossed crutches.

Elric felt beneath his ragged robes for the hilt of his sword and with his left hand pushed at the door. It squeaked open a fraction. They looked about them to see if anyone had heard the sound, but the square was as still as it had been.

More pressure. Another squeak. And now they could squeeze their bodies through the aperture.

They stood in Urish's hall. Braziers of garbage gave off faint light. Oily smoke curled towards the rafters. They saw the dim outlines of the dais at the far end and on the dais stood Urish's huge, crude throne. The hall seemed deserted, but Elric's hand did not leave the hilt of the Black Sword.

He stopped as he heard a sound, but it was a great,
black rat scuttling across the floor.

Silence again.

Elric moved forward, step by cautious step, along
the length of the slimy hall, Moonglum behind him.

Elric's spirits began to rise, as they neared the throne.
Perhaps Urish had, after all, grown complacent of his
strength. He would open the trunk beneath the throne,
remove his ring and then they would leave the city
and be away before dawn, riding across country to join
the caravan of Rackhir the Red Archer on its way to
Tanelorn.

He began to relax but his step was just as cautious.
Moonglum had paused, cocking his head to one side as
if hearing something.

Elric turned. "What is it you hear?"

"Possibly nothing. Or maybe one of those great rats
we saw earlier. It is just that—"

A silver-blue radiance burst out from behind the
grotesque throne and Elric flung up his left hand to
protect his eyes, trying to disentangle his sword from
his rags.

Moonglum yelled and began to run for the door, but
even when Elric put his back to the light he could not
see. Stormbringer moaned in its scabbard as if in rage.
Elric tugged at it, but felt his limbs grow weaker and
weaker. From behind him came a laugh which he recognised. A second laugh—almost a throaty cough—
joined it.

His sight came back but now he was held by clammy
hands and when he saw his captors he shuddered.
Shadowy creatures of limbo held him—ghouls summoned by sorcery. Their dead faces smiled but their
dead eyes remained dead. Elric felt the heat and the
strength leaving his body and it was as if the ghouls
sucked it from him. He could almost feel his vitality
travelling from his own body to theirs.

Again the laugh. He looked up at the throne and
saw emerging from behind it the tall, saturnine figure of

Theleb K'aarna, whom he had left for dead near the castle of Kaneloon a few months since.

Theleb K'aarna smiled in his curling beard as Elric struggled in the grasp of the ghouls. Now from the other side of the throne came the filthy carcass of Urish the Seven-fingered, the cleaver Hackmeat cradled in his left arm.

Elric could barely hold his head up as the ghouls' cold flesh absorbed his strength, but he smiled at his own foolishness. He had been right in suspecting a trap, but wrong in entering it so poorly prepared.

And where was Moonglum? Had he deserted him? The little Eastlander was nowhere to be seen.

Urish swaggered round the throne and sprawled his begrimed person in it, placing Hackmeat so that it lay across the arms. His pale, beady eyes stared hard at Elric.

Theleb K'aarna remained standing by the side of the throne, but triumph flamed in his eyes like Imrryr's own funeral fires.

"Welcome back to Nadsokor," wheezed Urish, scratching himself between the legs. "You have returned to make amends, I take it."

Elric shivered as the cold in his bones increased. Stormbringer stirred at his side but it could only help him if he drew it with his own hands. He knew he was dying.

"I have come to regain my property," he said through chattering teeth. "My ring."

"Ah! The Ring of Kings. It was yours, was it? My girl mentioned something of that."

"You sent her to steal it!"

Urish sniggered. "I'll not deny it. But I did not expect the White Wolf of Imrryr to step so easily into my trap."

"He would have stepped out again if you had not that amateur magic-maker's spells to help you!"

Theleb K'aarna glowered but then his face relaxed. "Are you not discomforted, then, by my ghouls?"

Elric was gasping as the last of the heat fled his bones.

He now could not stand, but hung in the hands of the dead creatures. Theleb K'aarna must have planned this for weeks, for it took many spells and pacts with the guardians of Limbo to bring such ghouls to Earth.

"And so I die," Elric murmured. "Well, I suppose I do not care. . . ."

Urish raised his ruined features in what was a parody of pride. "You do not die yet, Elric of Melniboné. The sentence has yet to be passed! The formalities must be suffered! By my cleaver Hackmeat I must sentence you for your crimes against Nadsokor and against the Sacred Hoard of King Urish!"

Elric hardly heard him as his legs collapsed altogether and the ghouls tightened their grip on him.

Dimly he was aware of the beggar rabble shuffling into the hall. Doubtless they had all been waiting for this. Had Moonglum died at their hands when he fled the hall?

"Put his head up!" Theleb K'aarna instructed his dead servants. "Let him see Urish, King of All Beggars, make his just decree!"

Elric felt a cold hand beneath his chin and his head was raised so he could watch, through misting eyes, as Urish stood up and grasped the cleaver Hackmeat in his four-fingered hand, stretching it towards the smoky ceiling.

"Elric of Melniboné thou art convicted of many crimes against the Ignoblest of the Ignoble—myself, King Urish of Nadsokor. Thou has offended King Urish's friend, that most pleasingly degenerate villain Theleb K'aarna—"

At this Theleb K'aarna pursed his lips, but did not interrupt.

"—and, moreover, did come a second time to the City of Beggars to repeat your crimes. By my great cleaver Hackmeat, the symbol of my dignity and power, I condemnest thou to the Punishment of the Burning God!"

From all sides of the hall came the foul applause of the Beggar Court. Elric remembered a legend of

Nadsokor—that when the original population were first struck by the disease they summoned aid from Chaos— begging Chaos to cleanse the disease from the city— with fire if necessary. Chaos had played a joke upon these folk—sent the Burning God who had burned what was left of their possessions. A further summons to Law to help them had resulted in the Burning God's being imprisoned by Lord Donblas in the city. Having had enough of the Lords of the Higher Worlds the remnants of the citizens had abandoned their city. But was the Burning God still here in Nadsokor?

Faintly he still heard Urish's voice. "Take him to the labyrinth and give him to the Burning God!"

Theleb K'aarna spoke but Elric did not hear what he said, though he heard Urish's reply.

"His sword? How will that avail him against a Lord of Chaos? Besides, if the sword is released from the scabbard, who knows what will happen?"

Theleb K'aarna was evidently reluctant, by his tone, but at last agreed with Urish.

Now Theleb K'aarna's voice boomed commandingly. "Things of Limbo—release him! His vitality has been your reward! Now—begone!"

Elric fell to the muck on the flagstones but was now too weak to move as beggars came forward and lifted him up.

His eyes closed and his senses deserted him as he felt himself borne from the hall and heard the united voices of the wizard of Pan Tang and the King of the Beggars giving vent to their mocking triumph.

CHAPTER FOUR

Punishment of the Burning God

"By Narjhan's droppings he's cold!"

Elric heard the rasping voice of one of the beggars who carried him. He was still weak but some of the beggars' body heat had transferred itself to him and the chill of his bones was now by no means as intense.

"Here's the portal."

Elric forced his eyes open.

He was upside down but could see ahead of him through the gloom.

Something shimmered there.

It looked like the iridescent skin of some unearthly animal stretched across the arch of the tunnel.

He was jerked backwards as the beggars swung his body and hurled it towards the shimmering skin.

He struck it.

It was viscous.

It clung to him and he felt it was absorbing him. He tried to struggle but was still far too weak. He was sure that he was being killed.

But after long minutes he was through it and had struck stone and lay gasping in the blackness of the tunnel.

This must be the labyrinth of which Urish had spoken.

Trembling, he tried to rise, using his scabbarded sword as a support. It took him some time to get up but at last he could lean against the curving wall.

He was surprised. The stones seemed to be hot. Perhaps it was because he was so cold and in reality the stones were of normal heat?

Even this speculation seemed to weary him. Whatever the nature of the heat it was welcome. He pressed his back harder against the stones.

As their heat passed into his body he felt a sensation almost of ecstacy and he drew a deep breath. Strength was returning slowly.

"Gods," he murmured, "even the snows of the Lormyrian steppe could not compare with such a great cold."

He drew another deep breath and coughed.

Then he realised that the drug he had swallowed was beginning to wear off.

He wiped his mouth with the back of his hand and spat out saliva. Something of the stink of Nadsokor had entered his nostrils.

He stumbled back towards the portal. The peculiar stuff still shimmered there. He pressed his hand against it and it gave reluctantly but then held firm. He leant his whole weight on it but it would still not give any further. It was like a particularly tough membrane but it was not flesh. Was this the stuff with which the Lords of Law had sealed off the tunnel, entrapping their enemy, the Lord of Chaos? The only light in the tunnel came from the membrane itself.

"By Arioch, I'll turn the tables on the Beggar King," Elric murmured. He threw back his rags and put his hand on Stormbringer's pommel. The blade purred as a cat might purr. He drew the sword from its scabbard and it began to sing a low, satisfied song. Now Elric hissed as its power flowed up his arm and into his body. Stormbringer was giving him the strength he needed—but he knew that Stormbringer must be paid soon, must taste blood and souls and thus replenish its energy. He aimed a great blow at the shimmering wall. "I'll hack down this portal and release the Burning God upon Nadsokor! Strike true, Stormbringer! Let flame come to devour the filth that is this city!"

But Stormbringer howled as it bit into the membrane and it was held fast. No rent appeared in the stuff. Instead Elric had to tug with all his might to get the sword free. He withdrew, panting.

"The portal was made to withstand the efforts of Chaos," Elric murmured. "My sword's useless against it. And so, unable to go back I must, perforce, go forward." Stormbringer in hand he turned and began to make his way along the passage. He took one turn and then another and then a third and the light had disappeared completely. He reached for his pouch where his flint and tinder were kept, but the beggars had cut that from his belt as they carried him. He decided to retrace his steps. But by now he was deeply within the labyrinth and he could not find the portal.

"No portal—but no God, it seems. Mayhap there's another exit from this place. If it's blocked by a door of wood, then Stormbringer will soon carve me a path to freedom."

And so he pressed further into the labyrinth, taking a hundred twists and turns in the darkness before he paused again.

He had noticed that he was growing warmer. Now, instead of feeling horribly cold, he felt uncomfortably hot. He was sweating. He removed some of the upper layers of his rags and stood in his own shirt and breeks. He had begun to thirst.

Another turning and he saw light ahead.

"Well, Stormbringer, perhaps we are free after all!"

He began to run towards the source of the light. But it was not daylight, neither was it the light from the portal. This was firelight—of brands, perhaps.

He could see the sides of the tunnel quite clearly in the firelight. Unlike the masonry in the rest of Nadsokor, this was free of filth—a plain, grey stone stained by the red light.

The source of the light was around the next bend. But the heat had grown greater and his flesh stung as the sweat sprang from his pores.

"AAH!"

A great voice suddenly filled the tunnel as Elric

rounded the bend and saw the fire leaping not thirty yards distant.

"AAH! AT LAST!"

The voice came from the fire.

And Elric knew he had found the Burning God.

"I have no quarrel with you, my lord of Chaos!" he called. "I, too, serve Chaos!"

"But I must eat," came the voice. "CHECKALAKH MUST EAT!"

"I am poor food for one such as you," Elric said reasonably, putting both his hands around Stormbringer's hilt and taking a step backward.

"Aye, beggar, that thou art—but thou art the only food they send!"

"I'm no beggar!"

"Beggar or not, Checkalakh will devour thee!"

The flames shook and a shape began to be made of them. It was a human shape but comprised entirely of flame. Flickering hands of fire stretched out towards Elric.

And Elric turned.

And Elric ran.

And Checkalakh, the Burning God, came fast as a flash fire behind him.

Elric felt pain in his shoulder and he smelled burning cloth. He increased his speed, having no notion of where he ran.

And still the Burning God pursued him.

"Stop, mortal! It is futile! Thou canst not escape Checkalakh of Chaos!"

Elric shouted back in desperate humour. "I'll be no one's roast pork!" His step began to falter. "Not—not even a god's!"

Like the roar of flames up a chimney, Checkalakh replied, "Do not defy me, mortal! It is an honour to feed a god!"

Both the heat and the effort of running were exhausting Elric. A plan of sorts had formed in his brain when he had first encountered the Burning God. That was why he had started to run.

But now, as Checkalakh came on, he was forced to turn.

"Thou art somewhat feeble for so mighty a Lord of Chaos," he panted, readying his sword.

"My long sojourn here has weakened me," Checkalakh replied, "else I would have caught thee ere now! But catch thee I will! And devour thee I must!"

Stormbringer whined its defiance at the enfeebled Chaos God and blade struck out at flaming head and gashed the god's right cheek so that paler fire flickered there and something ran up the black blade and into Elric's heart so that he trembled in a mixture of terror and joy as some of the Burning God's lifeforce entered him.

Eyes of flame stared at the Black Sword and then at Elric. Brows of flame furrowed and Checkalakh halted.

"Thou art no ordinary beggar, 'tis true!"

"I am Elric of Melniboné and I bear the Black Sword. Lord Arioch is my master—a more powerful entity than you, Lord Checkalakh."

Something akin to misery passed across the god's fiery countenance. "Aye—there are many more powerful than me, Elric of Melniboné."

Elric wiped sweat from his face. He drew in great gulps of burning air. "Then why—why not combine your strength with mine. Together we can tear down the portal and take vengeance on those who have conspired to bring us together."

Checkalakh shook his head and little tongues of fire fell from it. "The portal will only open when I am dead. So it was decreed when Lord Donblas of Law imprisoned me here. Even if we were successful in destroying the portal—it would result in my death. Therefore, most powerful of mortals, I must fight thee and eat thee."

And again Elric began to run, desperately seeking the portal, knowing that the only light he could hope to find in the labyrinth came from the Burning God himself. Even if he were to defeat the god, he would still be trapped in the complex maze.

And then he saw it. He was back at the place where he had been thrown through the membrane.

"It is only possible to enter my prison through the portal, not leave it!" called Checkalakh.

"I'm aware of that!" Elric took a firmer grip on Stormbringer and turned to face the thing of flame.

Even as his sword swung back and forth, parrying every attempt of the Burning God's to seize him, Elric felt sympathy for the creature. He had come in answer to the summonings of mortals and he had been imprisoned for his pains.

But Elric's clothes had begun to smoulder now and even though Stormbringer supplied him with energy every time it struck Checkalakh the heat itself was beginning to overwhelm him. He sweated no more. Instead his skin felt dry and about to split. Blisters were forming on his white hands. Soon he would be able to hold the blade no longer.

"Arioch!" he breathed. "Though this creature be a fellow Lord of Chaos, aid me to defeat him!"

But Arioch lent him no extra strength. He had already learned from his patron demon that greater things were being planned on and above the Earth and that Arioch had little time for even the most favourite of his mortal charges.

Yet, from habit, still Elric murmured Arioch's name as he swept the sword so that it struck first Checkalakh's burning hands and then his burning shoulder and more of the god's energy entered him.

It seemed to Elric that even Stormbringer was beginning to burn and the pain in his blistered hands grew so great that it was at last the only sensation of which he was aware. He staggered back against the iridescent membrane and felt its fleshlike texture on his back. The ends of his long hair were beginning to smoke and large areas of his clothes had completely charred.

Was Checkalakh failing, though? The flames burned

less brightly and there was an expression of resignation beginning to form on the face of fire.

Elric drew on his pain as his only source of strength and he made the pain take the sword and bring it back over his head and he made the pain bring Stormbringer down in a massive blow aimed at the god's head.

And even as the blow descended the fire began to die. Then Stormbringer had struck and Elric yelled as an enormous wave of energy poured into his body and knocked him backwards so that the sword fell from his hand and he felt that his flesh could not contain what it now held. He rolled, moaning, on the floor and he kicked at the air, raising his twisted, blistered hands to the roof as if in supplication to some being who had the power to stop what was happening to him. There were no tears in his eyes, for it seemed that even his blood had begun to boil out of him.

"Arioch! Save me!" He was shuddering, screaming. "Arioch! Stop this thing happening to me!"

He was full of the energy of a god and the mortal frame was not meant to contain so much force.

"Aaaah! Take it from me!"

He became aware of a calm, beautiful face looking down upon him as he writhed. He saw a tall man—much taller than himself—and he knew that this was no mortal at all, but a god.

"It is over!" said a pure, sweet voice.

And, though the creature did not move, soft hands seemed to caress him and the pain began to diminish and the voice continued to speak.

"Long centuries ago, I, Lord Donblas the Justice Maker, came to Nadsokor to free it from the grip of Chaos. But I came too late. Evil brought more evil, as evil will, and I could not interfere too much with the affairs of mortals, for we of Law have sworn to let mankind make its own destiny if that is possible. Yet the Cosmic Balance swings now like the pendulum of a clock with a broken spring and terrible forces are at work on the Earth. Thou, Elric, art a servant of Chaos —yet thou hast served Law more than once. It has been said that the destiny of mankind rests within thee and that may be true. Thus, I aid thee—though I do so against mine own oath. . . ."

And Elric closed his eyes and felt at peace for the first time that he remembered.

The pain had gone, but great energy still filled him. When he opened his eyes again there was no beautiful face looking down on him and the scintillating membrane which had covered the archway had disappeared. Nearby Stormbringer lay and he sprang up and seized the sword, returning it to his scabbard. He noticed that the blisters had left his hands and that even his clothes were no longer charred.

Had he dreamed it all—or most of it?

He shook his head. He was free. He was strong. He had his sword with him. Now he would return to the hall of King Urish and take his vengeance both on Nadsokor's ruler and Theleb K'aarna.

He heard a footfall and withdrew into the shadows. Light filtered into the tunnel from gaps in the roof and it was plain that at this point it was close to the surface. A figure appeared and he recognised it at once.

"Moonglum!"

The little Eastlander grinned in relief and sheathed his swords. "I came here to aid you if I could, but I see you need no aid from me!"

"Not here. The Burning God is no more. I'll tell you of that later. What became of you?"

"When I realised we were in a trap I ran for the door, deciding it would be best if one of us were free and I knew it was you they wanted. But then I saw the door opening and realised they had been waiting there all along." Moonglum wrinkled his nose and dusted at the rags he still wore. "Thus I came to find myself lying at the bottom of one of those heaps of garbage littered about Urish's hall. I dived into it and stayed there, listening to what passed. As soon as I could, I found this tunnel, planning to help you however I could."

"And where are Urish and Theleb K'aarna now?"

"It appears that they go to make good Theleb K'aarna's bargain with Urish. Urish was not altogether happy with the plan to lure you here for he fears your power—"

"He has reason to! Now!"

"Aye. Well, it seems that Urish had heard what we had heard, that the caravan for Tanelorn was on its way back to that city. Urish has knowledge of Tanelorn —though not much, I gather—and fosters an unreasoning hatred for the place, perhaps because it is the opposite of what Nadsokor is."

"They plan to attack Rackhir's caravan?"

"Aye—and Theleb K'aarna is to summon creatures from Hell to ensure that their attack is successful. Rackhir has no sorcery to speak of, I believe."

"He served Chaos once, but no more—those who dwell in Tanelorn can have no supernatural masters."

"I gathered as much from the conversation."

"When do they make this attack?"

"They have gone already—almost as soon as they had dealt with you. Urish is impatient."

"It is unlike the beggars to make a direct attack on a caravan."

"They do not always have a powerful wizard for an ally."

"True." Elric frowned. "My own powers of sorcery are limited without the Ring of Kings upon my hand. Its supernatural qualities identify me as a true member of the Royal Line of Melniboné—the line which made so many bargains with the elementals. First I must recover my ring and then we go at once to aid Rackhir."

Moonglum glanced at the floor. "They said something of protecting Urish's Hoard in his absence. There may be a few armed men in the hall."

Elric smiled. "Now that we are prepared and now I have the strength of the Burning God in me, I think we shall be able to deal with a whole army, Moonglum."

Moonglum brightened. "Then I'll lead the way back to the hall. Come. This passage will take us to a door which is let into the side of the hall, near the throne."

They began to run along the passage until they came
at length to the door Moonglum had mentioned. Elric
did not pause but drew his sword and flung the door
open. It was only when he was in the hall that he
stopped. Daylight now lit the gloomy place, but it was
again deserted. No sword-bearing beggars awaited them.

Instead, there sat in Urish's throne a fat, scaly thing
of yellow and green and black. Brown bile dripped
from its grinning snout and it raised one of its many
paws in a mockery of a salute.

"Greetings," it hissed, "and beware—for I am the
guardian of Urish's treasure."

"A thing of Hell," Elric said. "A demon raised by
Theleb K'aarna. He has been brewing his spells for a
long time, methinks, if he can command so many foul
servants." He frowned and weighed Stormbringer in
his hand but, oddly, the blade did not seem to hunger
for battle.

"I warn thee," hissed the demon, "I cannot be slain
by a sword—not even that sword. It is my
wardpact. . . ."

"What is that?" whispered Moonglum, eying the
demon warily.

"He is of a race of demons used by all with sorcerous
power. He is a guardian. He will not attack unless
himself attacked. He is virtually invulnerable to mortal
weapons and, in his case, he has a ward against swords
—be they supernatural or no. If we attempted to slay
him with our swords, we should be struck down by all
the powers of Hell. We could not possibly survive."

"But you have just destroyed a god! A demon is
nothing compared with that!"

"A weak god," Elric reminded him. "And this is a
strong demon—for he is a representative of all demons
who would mass with him to preserve his wardpact."

"Is there no chance of defeating him?"

"If we are to help Rackhir, there is no reason for
trying. We must get to our horses and try to warn the
caravan. Later, perhaps, we can return and think of
some sorcery which will aid us against the demon."

Elric bowed sardonically to the demon and returned his salute. "Farewell unlovely one. May your master not return to release you and thus ensure you squat in this filth forever!"

The demon slobbered in rage. "My master is Theleb K'aarna—one of the most powerful sorcerers amongst your kind."

Elric shook his head. "Not my kind. I shall be slaying him soon and you will be left there until I discover the means of destroying you."

Somewhat pettishly, the demon folded its multitude of arms and closed its eyes.

Elric and Moonglum strode through the muck-strewn hall towards the door.

They were close to vomiting by the time they reached the steps leading into the forum. The rest of Elric's potions had been taken when his purse was taken and they had no protection now against the stink. Moonglum spat on the steps as they descended into the square and then he looked up and drew his two swords in a cross-arm motion.

"Elric!"

Some dozen beggars were rushing at them, bearing an array of clubs, axes and knives.

Elric laughed. "Here's a titbit for you, Stormbringer!" He drew his sword and began to swing the howling blade around his head, moving implacably towards the beggars. Almost immediately two of their number broke and ran, but the rest came in a rush at the pair.

Elric brought the sword lower and took a head from its shoulders and had bitten deep into the next man's shoulder before the first's blood had begun to spout.

Moonglum darted in with his two slim swords and engaged two of the beggars at the same time. Elric stabbed at another and the man screamed and danced, clutching at the blade which remorselessly drew out his soul and his life.

Stormbringer was singing a sardonic song now and three of the surviving beggars dropped their weapons and were off across the square as Moonglum neatly took both his opponents simultaneously in their hearts and Elric hacked down the rest of the rabble as they shouted and groaned for mercy.

Elric sheathed Stormbringer, looked down at the crimson ruin he had caused, wiped his lips as a man might who had just enjoyed a fine meal, caused Moonglum to shudder, and clapped his friend on the shoulder.

"Come—let's to Rackhir's aid!"

As Moonglum followed the albino, he reflected that Elric had absorbed more than just the Burning God's life force in the encounter in the labyrinth. Much of the callousness of the Lords of Chaos was in him today.

Today Elric seemed a true warrior of ancient Melniboné.

CHAPTER FIVE

Things Which Are Not Women

       The beggars had been too absorbed in their triumph over the albino and their plans for their attack on the caravan of Tanelorn to think to seek the mounts on which Elric and Moonglum had come to Nadsokor.

They found the horses where they had left them the previous night. The superb Shazarian steeds were cropping the grass as if they had been waiting only a few minutes.

They climbed into their saddles and soon were riding as fast as the fleet horses could carry them—North-north-east to the point the caravan was logically due to reach.

Shortly after noon they had found it—a long sprawl of waggons and horses, awnings of gay, rich silks, brightly decorated harness, it stretched across the floor of a shallow valley. And surrounding it on all sides was the squalid and motley beggar army of King Urish of Nadsokor.

Elric and Moonglum reined in their horses when they reached the brow of the hill and they watched.

Theleb K'aarna and King Urish were not immediately visible and at last Elric saw them on the opposite hill. By the way in which the sorcerer was stretching out his arms to the deep blue sky Elric guessed he was already summoning the aid he had promised Urish.

Below Elric saw a flash of red and knew that it must be the scarlet garb of the Red Archer. Peering closer he saw one or two other shapes he recognised—Brut of Lashmar with his blond hair and his huge, burly body almost dwarfing his warhorse; Carkan, once of Pan Tang himself, but now dressed in the chequered cloak and fur cap of the barbarians of Southern Ilmiora. Rackhir himself had been a Warrior Priest from Moonglum's country beyond the Weeping Waste, but all these men had foresworn their gods to go to live in peaceful Tanelorn where, it was said, even the greatest Lords of the Higher Worlds could not enter— Eternal Tanelorn, which had stood for uncountable cycles and would outlive the Earth herself.

Knowing nothing of Theleb K'aarna's plan Rackhir was plainly not too worried by the appearance of the beggar rabble which was as poorly armed as those Elric and Moonglum had fought in Nadsokor.

"We must ride through their army to reach Rackhir now," Moonglum said.

Elric nodded but he made no move. He was watching the distant hill where Theleb K'aarna continued his incantation, hoping that he might guess what kind of aid the sorcerer was summoning.

A moment later Elric yelled and spurred his horse down the hill at a gallop. Moonglum was almost as startled as the beggars as he followed his friend into the thick of the ragged horde, slashing this way and that with the longest of his swords.

Elric's Stormbringer emitted black radiance as it carved a bloody path through the beggar army, leaving in its wake a mess of dismembered bodies, entrails and dead, horrified eyes.

Moonglum's horse was splashed with blood to the shoulder and it snorted and balked at following the white-skinned demon with the howling black blade, but Moonglum, afraid that the beggar ranks would close, forced it on until at last they were both riding towards the caravan and someone was yelling Elric's name.

It was Rackhir the Red Archer, clothed in scarlet from head to foot, with a red bone bow in his hand and a red quiver of crimson-fletched arrows on his back. On his head was a scarlet skull cap decorated with a single scarlet feather. His face was weather-beaten and all but fleshless. He had fought with Elric before the Fall of Imrryr and together they had discovered the Black Swords. Rackhir had gone on to seek Tanelorn and find it at last.

. Elric had not seen Rackhir since then. Now he noted an enviable look of peace in the archer's eyes. Rackhir had once been a Warrior Priest in the Eastlands, serving Chaos, but now he served nothing but his tranquil Tanelorn.

"Elric! Have you come to help us send Urish and his beggars back to where they came from?" Rackhir was laughing, evidently pleased to see his old friend. "And Moonglum! When did you two meet? I have not seen thee since I left the Eastlands!"

Moonglum grinned. "Much has come to pass since those days, Rackhir."

Rackhir rubbed at his aquiline nose. "Aye—so I've heard."

Elric dismounted swiftly. "No time for reminiscence now, Rackhir. You're in greater danger than you know."

"What? When did the beggar rabble of Nadsokor offer anything to fear? Look how poorly armed they are!"

"They have a sorcerer with them—Theleb K'aarna of Pan Tang. See—that's him on yonder hill."

Rackhir frowned. "Sorcery. These days I've little guard against that. How good is the sorcerer, do you know?"

"He is one of the most powerful in Pan Tang."

"And the wizards of Pan Tang almost equal your folk, Elric, in their skills."

"I fear he more than equals me at present, for my Actorios Ring has been stolen from me by Urish."

Rackhir looked strangely at Elric, noting something in the albino's face which he had evidently not seen there when they last parted. "Well," he said, "we shall have to defend ourselves as best we can. . . ."

"If you cut loose your horses so that all your folk could be mounted we might be able to escape before

Theleb K'aarna invokes whatever supernatural aid it is he seeks." Elric nodded as the giant, Brut of Lashmar, rode up grinning at him. Brut had been a hero in Lashmar before he had disgraced himself.

Rackhir shook his head. "Tanelorn needs the provisions we carry."

"Look," said Moonglum quietly.

On the hill where Theleb K'aarna had been standing there had now appeared a billowing cloud of redness, like blood in clear water.

"He is successful," Rackhir murmured. "Brut! Let all be mounted. We've no time to prepare further defences, but we'll have the advantage of being on horseback when they attack."

Brut thundered off, yelling at the men of Tanelorn. They began to unharness the wagon horses and ready their weapons.

The cloud of redness above was beginning to disperse and out of it shapes were emerging. Elric tried to distinguish the shapes but could not at that distance. He climbed back into his saddle as the horsemen of Tanelorn now formed themselves into groups which would, when the attack came, race through the unmounted beggars striking swiftly and passing on. Rackhir waved to Elric and went to join one of these divisions. Elric and Moonglum found themselves at the head of a dozen warriors armed with axes, pikes and lances.

Then Urish's voice cawed out over the waiting silence.

"Attack, my beggars! They are doomed!"

The beggar rabble began to move down the sides of the valley. Rackhir raised his sword as the signal to his men. Then the first groups of cavalry rode out from the caravan, straight at the advancing beggars.

Rackhir replaced his blade and took up his bow. From where he sat on his horse he began to send arrow after arrow into the beggar ranks.

There was shouting everywhere now as the warriors of Tanelorn met their foes, driving wedges everywhere in their mass.

Elric saw Carkan's chequered cape in the midst of a sea of rags, filthy limbs, clubs and knives. He saw Brut's great blond head towering over a cluster of human filth.

And Moonglum said: "Such creatures as these are unfit opponents for the warriors of Tanelorn."

Elric pointed grimly up the hill. "Perhaps they'll prefer their new foes."

Moonglum gasped. "They are women!"

Elric drew Stormbringer from its scabbard. "They are not women. They are Elenoin. They come from the Eighth Plane—and neither are they human. You will see."

"You recognize them?"

"My ancestors fought them once."

A strange, shrill ululation reached their ears now. It came from the hillside where Theleb K'aarna's figure could again be seen. It came from the shapes which Moonglum was sure were women. Red-haired women whose tresses fell almost to their knees and covered their otherwise completely naked bodies. They danced down the hill towards the besieged caravan and they whirled swords about their heads which must have been over five feet long.

"Theleb K'aarna is clever," Elric muttered. "The warriors of Tanelorn will hesitate before striking at women. And while they hesitate the Elenoin will rip and slash and slay them."

Rackhir had already seen the Elenoin and he, too, recognised them for what they were. "Do not be deceived, men!" he called. "These creatures are demons!" He glanced across at Elric and there was a look of resignation on his face. He knew the power of the Elenoin. He spurred his horse towards the albino. "What can we do, Elric?"

Elric sighed. "What can mortals do against the Elenoin?"

"Have you no sorcery?"

"With the Ring of Kings I could summon the Grahluk, perhaps. They are the ancient enemies of the

Elenoin. Theleb K'aarna has already made a gateway from the Eighth Plane."

"Could you not try to call the Grahluk?" Rackhir begged.

"While I tried my sword would not be aiding you. I think Stormbringer is more use today than spells."

Rackhir shuddered and turned his horse away to order his men to re-form their ranks. He knew now that they were all to die.

And now the beggars fell back, as horrified by the Elenoin as were the men of Tanelorn.

Still singing their shrill, chill song, the Elenoin lowered their swords and spread out along the hill, each one smiling at them.

"How can they . . . ?" Then Moonglum saw their eyes. They were huge, orange, animal eyes. "Oh, by the Gods!" And then he saw their teeth—long, pointed teeth which glinted like metal.

The horsemen of Tanelorn fell back to the waggons in a long, ragged line. Horror, despair, uncertainty was on every face save Elric's—and on his face was a look of grim anger. His crimson eyes smouldered as he held Stormbringer across his saddle pommel and regarded the demon women, the Elenoin.

The singing grew louder until it made their ears fill with sharp pain and made their stomachs turn. The Elenoin raised their slender arms and began to whirl their long swords about their heads again, staring at them all the while through beastlike, insensate eyes— malicious, unblinking eyes.

Then Carkan of Pan Tang, his fur cap askew, his chequered cloak billowing, gave a strangled yell and urged his heavy horse at them, his own sword waving.

"Back, demons! Back, spawn of hell!"

"Aaaaaaaah!" gasped the Elenoin in anticipation. "Eeeeeeeh!" they sang.

And Carkan was suddenly in the midst of a dozen slender, slashing swords and he and his horse were cut all to tiny morsels of flesh which lay in a heap at the feet of the Elenoin. And their laughter filled the valley

as some of them bent to pop the flesh into their fanged
mouths.

A groan of horror and hatred went up from the
ranks of Tanelorn then and screaming men, hysterical
with fear and disgust, began to fling themselves at the
Elenoin who laughed the more and whirled their sharp
swords.

Stormbringer murmured as it seemed to hear the
sounds of battle, but Elric did not move as he stared
at the scene. He knew that the Elenoin would kill all
as they had killed Carkan.

Moonglum moaned. "Elric—there must be some
sorcery against them!"

"There is! But I cannot summon the Grahluk!"
Elric's chest was heaving and his brain was in turmoil.
"I cannot, Moonglum!"

"For the sake of Tanelorn, you must try!"

Then Elric was riding forward, Stormbringer howling, riding at the Elenoin and screaming Arioch's name
as his ancestors had screamed it since the founding of
Imrryr!

"Arioch! Arioch! Blood and souls for my Lord
Arioch!"

He parried the whirling blade of an Elenoin and
glared into the bestial eyes as Stormbringer sent a shudder down his arm. He struck and his own blow was
parried by the demon that was not a woman. Red hair
swung and curled around his throat. He hacked at it
and it loosened its grip. He thrust at the naked body
and the Elenoin danced aside. Another whistling blow
from the slim sword and he flung himself backwards
to avoid it, toppling from his saddle and springing instantly to his feet to parry a second attack, gripped
Stormbringer in both hands and stepped forward under
the blade to plunge the Black Sword into the smooth
belly. The Elenoin shouted with anger and green foulness billowed from the wound. The Elenoin fell, still
glaring and snarling, still living. Elric chopped at the
neck and the head sprang off, its hair thrashing at him.
He dashed forward, picked up the head and began to

run up the hill to where the beggars were gathered, watching the destruction of Tanelorn's warriors. As he approached the beggars broke and began to run, but he caught one in the back with his blade. The man fell, tried to crawl on, but his twisted knees would not support him and he collapsed into the stained grass. Elric picked the wretch up and flung him over his shoulder. Then he turned and began to run down the hill back to the camp. The warriors of Tanelorn were fighting well, but half their number had already been slain by the Elenoin. Almost unbelievably there were also several Elenoin corpses on the field.

Elric saw Moonglum defending himself with both swords. He saw Rackhir, still mounted, shouting orders to his men. He saw Brut of Lashmar in the thick of the fight. But he ran on until he stood behind one of the waggons and had dropped both his bloody bundles to the ground. With his sword he split open the twitching body of the beggar and he gathered up the hair of the Elenoin and soaked it in the man's blood.

Again he stood upright, looking towards the west, with the bloody hair in one hand and Stormbringer in the other. He raised both sword and head and began to speak in the ancient High Speech of Melniboné.

Held to the West and soaked in the blood of an enemy, the hair of an Elenoin must be used to summon the enemies of the Elenoin—the Grahluk. He remembered the words he had read in his father's ancient grimoire.

And now the invocation:

> *Grahluk come and Grahluk slay!*
> *Come kill thine ancient enemy!*
> *Make this thy victory day.*

All the strength of the Burning God was leaving him as he used the energy to perform the invocation. And perhaps without the Ring of Kings he was wasting that strength for nothing.

Grahluk speed without delay!
Come kill thine ancient enemy!
Make this thy vengeance day.

The spell was far less complex than many he had used in the past. Yet it took as much from him as any spell ever had.

"Grahluk, I summon thee! Grahluk, here you may take vengeance on your foes!"

Many cycles since, the Elenoin were said to have driven the Grahluk from their lands in the Eighth Plane and the Grahluk sought revenge now at every opportunity.

All around Elric the air shivered and turned brown, then green, then black.

"Grahluk! Come destroy the Elenoin!" Elric's voice was weakening. "Grahluk—the gateway is made!"

And now the ground trembled and strange winds blew at the blood-soaked hair of the Elenoin and the air became thick and purple and Elric fell to his knees, still croaking the invocation.

"Grahluk . . ."

A shuffling sound. A grunting noise. The stink of something unnameable.

The Grahluk had come. They were apelike creatures as bestial as the Elenoin. They carried nets and ropes and shields. Once, it was said, both Grahluk and Elenoin had had intelligence—had been part of the same species which had devolved and divided.

They moved out of the purple mist in their scores and they stood looking at Elric who was still on his knees. Elric pointed at where the remaining warriors of Tanelorn were still fighting the Elenoin.

"There . . ."

The Grahluk snorted with battle-greed and shambled towards the Elenoin.

The Elenoin saw them and their shrill wailing voices changed in quality as they retreated a short distance up the hill.

Elric forced himself to his feet and gasped: "Rackhir! Withdraw your warriors. The Grahluk will do their work now. . . ."

"You helped us after all!" Rackhir yelled, turning his horse. His clothes were all in tatters and there were a dozen wounds on his body.

They watched as the Grahluk's nets and nooses flashed towards the screaming Elenoin whose sword blows were stopped by the Grahluk shields. They watched as the Elenoin were crushed and throttled and parts of their entrails devoured by the grunting, apelike demons.

And when the last of the Elenoin was dead, the Grahluk picked up the fallen swords and reversed them and fell upon them.

Rackhir said: "They are killing themselves. Why?"

"They live only to destroy the Elenoin. Once that is done, they have nothing left for which to exist." Elric swayed and Rackhir and Moonglum caught him.

"See!" Moonglum laughed. "The beggars are running!"

"Theleb K'aarna," Elric muttered. "We must get Theleb K'aarna. . . ."

"Doubtless he has gone back with Urish to Nadsokor," Moonglum said.

"I must—I must retrieve the Ring of Kings."

"Plainly you can work your sorcery without it," Rackhir said.

"Can I?" Elric looked up and showed his face to Rackhir who lowered his eyes and nodded.

"We will help you get back your ring," Rackhir said quietly. "There'll be no more trouble from the beggars. We'll ride with you to Nadsokor."

"I had hoped you would." Elric climbed with difficulty into the saddle of a surviving horse and jerked at its reins, turning it towards the City of Beggars. "Perhaps your arrows will slay what my sword can-not. . . ."

"I do not understand you," Rackhir said.

Moonglum was mounting now. "We'll tell you on the way."

CHAPTER SIX

The Jesting Demon

Through the filth of Nadsokor now rode the warriors of Tanelorn.

Elric, Moonglum and Rackhir were at the head of the company but there was no ostentatious triumph in their demeanour. The riders looked neither to left nor to right and the beggars offered no threat now, not daring to attack but instead cowering into the shadows.

A potion of Rackhir's had helped Elric recover some of his strength and he no longer leaned over his horse's neck but sat upright as they crossed the forum, came to the palace of the Beggar King.

Elric did not pause. He rode his horse up the steps and into the gloomy hall.

"Theleb K'aarna!" Elric shouted.

His voice boomed through the hall, but Theleb K'aarna did not reply.

The braziers of garbage guttered in the wind from the opened door and threw a little more light on the dais at the end.

"Theleb K'aarna!"

But it was not Theleb K'aarna who knelt there. It was a wretched, ragged figure and it sprawled before the throne and it was sobbing, imploring, whining at something on the throne.

Elric walked his horse a little further into the hall and now he could see what occupied the throne.

Squatting in the great chair of black oak was the demon which had been there earlier. Its arms were folded and its eyes were shut and it seemed, somewhat

116

theatrically, to be ignoring the pleadings of the creature kneeling at its feet.

The others, also mounted, entered the hall now and together they rode up to the dais and stopped.

The kneeling figure turned its head and it was Urish. It gasped when it saw Elric and stretched out a maimed hand for its cleaver, abandoned some distance away.

Elric sighed.

"Do not fear me, Urish. I'm weary of blood-letting. I do not want your life."

The demon opened its eyes.

"Prince Elric, you have returned," it said. There seemed to be an indefinable difference in its tone.

"Aye. Where is your master?"

"I fear he has fled Nadsokor forever."

"And left you to sit here for eternity."

The demon inclined its head.

Urish put a grimy hand on Elric's leg. "Elric—help me! I must have my Hoard. It is everything! Destroy the demon and I will give you back the Ring of Kings."

Elric smiled. "You are generous, King Urish."

Tears streamed down the filth on Urish's ruined face. "Please, Elric, I beg thee. . . ."

"It is my intention to destroy the demon."

Urish looked nervously about him. "And aught else?"

"That decision lies with the men of Tanelorn whom you sought to rob and whose friends you caused to be slain in a most foul manner."

"It was Theleb K'aarna, not I!"

"And where is Theleb K'aarna now?"

"When you unleashed those ape things on our Elenoin he fled the field. He went towards the Varkalk River—towards Troos."

Without looking behind him Elric said, "Rackhir? Will you try the arrows now?"

There was the hum of a bowstring and an arrow struck the demon in the breast. It quivered there and the demon looked at it with mild interest, then breathed in deeply. As he breathed the arrow was drawn further into him and was eventually absorbed altogether.

"Aaah!" Urish scuttled for his cleaver. "It will not work!"

A second arrow sped from Rackhir's scarlet bow and it, too, was absorbed, as was the third.

Urish was gibbering now, waving his cleaver.

Elric warned him: "He has a wardpact against swords, King Urish!"

The demon rattled its scales. "Is that thing a sword, I wonder?"

Urish hesitated. Spittle ran down his chin and his red eyes rolled. "Demon—begone! I must have my Hoard —it is mine!"

The demon watched him sardonically.

With a yell of terror and anguish Urish flung himself at the demon, the cleaver Hackmeat swinging wildly. Its blade came down on the hell-thing's head, there was a sound like lightning striking metal and the cleaver shivered to pieces. Urish stood staring at the demon in quaking anticipation. Casually the demon reached out four of its hands and seized him. Its jaws opened wider than should have been possible, the bulk of the demon expanded until it was suddenly twice its original size. It brought the kicking Beggar King to its maw and suddenly there were only two legs waving from the mouth and then the demon gave a mighty swallow and there was nothing at all left of Urish of Nadsokor.

Elric shrugged. "Your wardpact is effective."

The demon smiled. "Aye, sweet Elric."

Now the tone of voice was very familiar. Elric looked narrowly at the demon. "You're no ordinary . . ."

"I hope not, most beloved of mortals."

Elric's horse reared and snorted as the demon's shape began to alter. There was a humming sound and black smoke coiled over the throne and then another figure was sitting there, its legs crossed. It had the shape of a man but it was more beautiful than any

mortal. It was a being of intense and majestic beauty—
unearthly beauty.

"Arioch!" Elric bowed his head before the Lord of
Chaos.

"Aye, Elric. I took the demon's place while you
were gone."

"But you have refused to aid me. . . ."

"There are larger affairs afoot, as I've told you.
Soon Chaos must engage with Law and such as Donblas will be dismissed to Limbo for eternity."

"You knew Donblas spoke to me in the labyrinth of
the Burning God?"

"Indeed I did. That was why I afforded myself the
time to visit your plane. I cannot have you patronised
by Donblas the Justice Maker and his humourless kind.
I was offended. Now I have shown you that my power
is greater than Law's." Arioch stared beyond Elric at
Rackhir, Brut, Moonglum and the rest who were protecting their eyes from his beauty. "Perhaps you fools
of Tanelorn now realise that it is better to serve Chaos!"

Rackhir said grimly: "I serve neither Chaos nor
Law!"

"One day you will be taught that neutrality is more
dangerous than side-taking, renegade!" The harmoni-
ous voice was now almost vicious.

"You cannot harm me," Rackhir said. "And if Elric
returns with us to Tanelorn, then he, too, may rid himself of your evil yoke!"

"Elric is of Melniboné. The folk of Melniboné all
serve Chaos—and are greatly rewarded. How else
would you have rid this throne of Theleb K'aarna's
demon?"

"Perhaps in Tanelorn Elric would have no need of
his Ring of Kings," Rackhir replied levelly.

There was a sound like rushing water, the boom of
thunder and Arioch's form began to grow larger. But
as it grew it also began to fade until there was nothing
left in the hall but the stench of its garbage.

Elric dismounted and ran to the throne. Reaching

under it he drew out dead Urish's chest and hacked it open with Stormbringer. The sword murmured as if resenting the menial work. Gems, gold, artifacts scattered through the muck as Elric sought his ring.

And then at last he held it up in triumph, replacing it on his finger. His step was lighter as he returned to his horse.

Moonglum had in the meantime dismounted and was scooping the best of the jewels into his pouch. He winked at Rackhir, who smiled.

"And now," Elric said, "I go to Troos to seek Theleb K'aarna there. I have still to take my vengeance upon him."

"Let him rot in Troos's sickly forest," Moonglum said.

Rackhir placed a hand on Elric's shoulder. "If Theleb K'aarna hates you so, he will find you again. Why waste your own time in the pursuit?"

Elric smiled slightly at his old friend. "You were ever clever in your arguments, Rackhir. And it is true that I am weary—both gods and demons have fallen to my blade in the little while since I came to Nadsokor."

"Come, rest in Tanelorn—peaceful Tanelorn, where even the greatest Lords of the Higher Worlds cannot come without permission."

Elric looked down at the ring on his finger. "Yet I have sworn Theleb K'aarna shall perish. . . ."

"There will be time yet to fulfil your oath."

Elric ran his hand through his milk-white hair and it seemed to his friends that there were tears in his crimson eyes.

"Aye," he said. "Aye. Time yet. . . ."

And they rode away from Nadsokor, leaving the beggars to brood in the stink and the foulness and regret that they had aught to do with sorcery or with Elric of Melniboné.

They rode for Eternal Tanelorn. Tanelorn, which

had welcomed and held all troubled wanderers who came upon it. All save one.

Doom-haunted, full of guilt, of sorrow, of despair, Elric of Melniboné prayed that this time Tanelorn might hold even him. . . .

BOOK THREE

Three Heroes with a Single Aim

". . . Elric, of all the manifestations of the Champion Eternal, was to find Tanelorn without effort. And of all those manifestations he was the only one to choose to leave that city of myriad incarnations . . ."

—*The Chronicle of the Black Sword*

CHAPTER ONE

Tanelorn Eternal

Tanelorn had taken many forms in her endless existence, but all those forms, save one, had been beautiful.

She was beautiful now, with the soft sunlight on her pastel towers and her curved turrets and domes. And banners flew from her spires, but they were not battle banners, for the warriors who had found Tanelorn and had stayed there were weary of war.

She had been here always. None knew when Tanelorn had been built, but some knew that she had existed before Time and would exist after the end of Time and that was why she was known as Eternal Tanelorn.

She had played a significant role in the struggles of many heroes and many gods and because she existed beyond Time she was hated by the Lords of Chaos who had more than once sought to destroy her. To the north of her lay the rolling plains of Ilmiora, a land where justice was known to prevail, and to the south of her lay desolation which was the Sighing Desert, endless wasteland over which hissed a constant wind. If Ilmiora represented Law, then the Sighing Desert certainly mirrored something of the barrenness of Ultimate Chaos. Those who dwelled in her had loyalty neither to Law nor to Chaos and they had chosen to have no part in the Cosmic Struggle which was waged continuously by the Lords of the Higher Worlds. There were no leaders and there were no followers in Tanelorn and her citizens lived in harmony with each other, even

though many had been warriors of great reputation
before they chose to stay there. But one of the most
admired citizens of Tanelorn, one who was often con-
sulted by the others, was Rackhir of the ascetic features who had once been a fierce warrior-priest in
P'hum where he had gained the name of the Red Archer
because his skill with a bow was great and he dressed
all in scarlet. His skill and his dress remained the
same, but his urge to fight had left him since he had
come to live in Tanelorn.

Close to the low west wall of the city lay a house of
two storeys surrounded by a lawn in which grew all
manner of wild flowers. The house was of pink and
yellow marble and, unlike most of the other dwellings
in Tanelorn, it had a tall, pointed roof. This was
Rackhir's house and Rackhir sat outside it now,
sprawled on a bench of plain wood while he watched
his guest pace the lawn. The guest was his old friend
the tormented albino Prince of Melniboné.

Elric wore a simple white shirt and britches of heavy
black silk. He had a band of the same black silk tied
around his head to keep back the mane of milk-white
hair which grew to his shoulders. His crimson eyes
were downcast as he paced and he did not look at
Rackhir at all.

Rackhir was unwilling to intrude upon his friend's
reverie and yet he hated to see Elric as he was now. He
had hoped that Tanelorn would comfort the albino,
drive away the ghosts and the doubts inhabiting his
skull, but it seemed that even Tanelorn could not
bring Elric tranquillity.

At last Rackhir broke his silence. "It has been a
month since you came to Tanelorn, my friend, yet still
you pace, still you brood."

Elric looked up with a slight smile. "Aye—still I
brood. Forgive me, Rackhir. I am a poor guest."

"What occupies your thoughts?"

"No particular subject. It seems that I cannot lose
myself in all this peace. Only violent action helps me

drive away my melancholy. I was not meant for Tanelorn, Rackhir."

"But violent action—or the results of it—produces further melancholy does it not?"

"It is true. It is the dilemma with which I live constantly. It is a dilemma I have been in since the burning of Imrryr—perhaps before."

"It is a dilemma known to all men, perhaps," Rackhir said. "At least to some degree."

"Aye—to wonder what purpose there is to one's existence and what point there is to purpose, even if it should be discovered."

"Tanelorn makes such problems seem meaningless to me," Rackhir told him. "I had hoped that you, too, would be able to dismiss them from your thoughts. Will you stay on in Tanelorn?"

"I have no other plans. I still thirst for vengeance upon Theleb K'aarna, but I now have no idea of his whereabouts. And, as you or Moonglum told me, Theleb K'aarna is sure to seek me out sooner or later. I remember once, when you first found Tanelorn, you suggested that I bring Cymoril here and forget Melniboné. I wish I had listened to you then, Rackhir, for now, I think, I would know peace and Cymoril's dead face would not be infesting my nights."

"You mentioned this sorceress who, you said, resembled Cymoril . . . ?"

"Myshella? She who is called Empress of the Dawn? I first saw her in a dream and when I left her side it was I who was in a dream. We served each other to achieve a common purpose. I shall not see her again."

"But if she—"

"I shall not see her again, Rackhir."

"As you say."

Once more the two friends fell silent and there was only birdsong and the splash of fountains in the air as Elric continued his pacing of the garden.

Some while later Elric suddenly turned on his heel

and went into the house followed by Rackhir's troubled gaze.

When Elric came out again he was wearing the great wide belt around his waist—the belt which supported the black scabbard containing his runesword Stormbringer. Over his shoulders was flung a cloak of white silk and he wore high boots.

"I go riding," he said. "I will go by myself into the Sighing Desert and I will ride until I am exhausted. Perhaps exercise is all I need."

"Be careful of the desert, my friend," Rackhir cautioned him. "It is a sinister and treacherous wilderness."

"I will be careful."

"Take the big golden mare. She is used to the desert and her stamina is legendary."

"Thank you. I will see you in the morning if I do not return earlier."

"Take care, Elric. I trust your remedy is successful and your melancholy disappears."

Rackhir's expression had little of relief in it as he watched his friend stride towards the near-by stables, his white cloak billowing behind him like a sea fog suddenly risen.

Then he heard the sound of Elric's horse as its hooves struck the cobbles of the street and Rackhir got to his feet to watch as the albino urged the golden mare into a canter and headed for the northern wall beyond which the great yellow waste of the Sighing Desert could be seen.

Moonglum came out of the house, a large apple in his hand, a scroll under his arm.

"Where goes Elric, Rackhir?"

"He looks for peace in the desert."

Moonglum frowned and bit thoughtfully into his apple. "He has sought peace in all other places and I fear he'll not find it there, either."

Rackhir nodded his agreement. "But it is my premonition he'll discover something else, for Elric is not always motivated by his own wishes. There are times when other forces work within him to make him take some fateful action."

"You think this is such a time?"

"It could be."

CHAPTER TWO

Return of a Sorceress

The sand rippled as the wind blew it so that the dunes seemed like waves in an almost petrified sea. Stark fangs of rock jutted here and there—the remains of mountain ranges which had been eroded by the wind. And a mournful sighing could just be heard, as if the sand remembered when it had been rock and the stones of cities and the bones of men and beasts and longed for its resurrection, sighed at the memory of its death.

Elric drew the cloak's cowl over his head to protect it from the fierce sun which hung in the steel-blue sky.

One day, he thought, I too shall know this peace of death and perhaps then I shall also regret it. He let the golden mare slow to a trot and took a sip of water from one of his canteens.

Now the desert surrounded him and it seemed infinite. Nothing grew. No animals lived there. There were no birds in the sky.

For some reason he shuddered and he had a presentiment of a moment in the future when he would be alone, as he was now, in a world even more barren than this desert, without even a horse for company. He shook off the thought, but it had left him so stunned that for a little while he achieved his ambition and did not brood upon his fate and his situation. The wind dropped slightly and the sighing became little more than a whisper.

Dazed, Elric fingered the pommel of his blade—Stormbringer, the Black Sword—for he associated his

130

presentiment with the weapon but could not tell why.
And it seemed to him that he heard an ironic note in
the murmuring of the wind. Or did the sound ema-
nate from his sword itself? He cocked his head, listening, but the sound became even less audible, as if
aware that he listened.

The golden mare began to climb the gentle slope of
a dune, stumbling once as her foot sank into deeper
sand. Elric concentrated on guiding her to firmer
ground.

Reaching the top of the dune he reined his horse
in. The desert dunes rolled on, broken only by the
occasional rock. He had it in mind then to ride on
and on until it would be impossible to return to
Tanelorn, until both he and his mount collapsed from
exhaustion and were eventually swallowed by the
sands. He pushed back his cowl and wiped sweat
from his brow.

Why not? he thought. Life was not bearable. He
would try death.

And yet would death deny him? Was he doomed to
live? It sometimes seemed so.

Then he considered the horse. It would not be fair
to sacrifice it to his desire. Slowly he dismounted.

The wind grew stronger and the sound of its sighing increased. Sand blew around Elric's booted feet.
It was a hot wind and it tugged at his voluminous
white cloak. The horse snorted nervously.

Elric looked towards the north east, towards the
edge of the world.

And he began to walk.

The horse whinnied enquiringly at him when he did
not call it, but he ignored the sound and had soon left
his mount behind him. He had not even bothered to
bring water with him. He flung back his cowl so that
the sun beat directly upon his head. His pace was
even, purposeful and he marched as if at the head of
an army.

Perhaps he did sense an army behind him—the

army of the dead, of all those friends and enemies whom he had slain in the course of his pointless search for a meaning to his existence.

And still one enemy remained alive. An enemy even stronger, even more malevolent than Theleb K'aarna—the enemy of his darker self, of that side of his nature which was symbolised by the sentient blade still resting at his hip. And when he died, then that enemy would also die. A force for evil would be removed from the world.

For several hours Elric of Melniboné tramped on through the Sighing Desert and gradually, as he had hoped, his sense of identity began to leave him so that it was almost as if he became one with the wind and the sand and, in so doing, was united at last with the world which had rejected him and which he had rejected.

Evening came, but he hardly noticed the sun's setting. Night fell, but he continued to march, unaware of the cold. Already he was weakening. He rejoiced in the weakness where previously he had fought to retain the strength he enjoyed only through the power of the Black Sword.

And sometime around midnight, beneath a pale moon, his legs buckled and he fell sprawling in the sand and lay there while the remains of his sensibilities left him.

"Prince Elric. My Lord?"

The voice was rich, vibrant, almost amused. It was a woman's voice and Elric recognised it. He did not move.

"Elric of Melniboné."

He felt a hand on his arm. She was trying to pull him upright. Rather than be dragged he raised himself with some difficulty to a sitting position. He tried to speak, but at first no words would come from his mouth which was dry and full of sand. She stood there as the dawn rose behind her and brightened her long black hair framing her beautiful features. She was dressed in a flowing gown of blue, green and gold and she was smiling.

As he cleared the sand from his mouth he shook his head, saying at last: "If I am dead, then I am still plagued by phantoms and illusions."

"I am no more illusion than anything else in this world. You are not dead, my lord."

"You are, in that case, many leagues from Castle Kaneloon, my lady. You have come from the other side of the world—from edge to edge."

"I have been seeking you, Elric."

"Then you have broken your word, Myshella, for when we parted you said that you would not see me again, that our fates had ceased to be twined."

"I thought then that Theleb K'aarna was dead— that our mutual enemy had perished in the Noose of Flesh." The sorceress spread her arms wide and it was almost as if the gesture summoned the sun, for it appeared over the horizon, suddenly. "Why did you walk thus in the desert, my lord?"

"I sought death."

"Yet you know it is not your destiny to die in such a way."

"I have been told as much but I do not *know* it, Lady Myshella. However," he stumbled upright and stood swaying before her, "I am beginning to suspect that it is so."

She came forward, bringing a goblet from beneath her robes. It was full to the brim with a cool, silvery liquid. "Drink," she said.

He did not lift his hands towards the cup. "I am not pleased to see you, Lady Myshella."

"Why? Because you are afraid to love me?"

"If it flatters you to think that—aye."

"It does not flatter me. I know you are reminded of Cymoril and that I made the mistake of letting Kaneloon become that which you most desire—before I understood that it is also what you most fear."

He lowered his head. "Be silent!"

"I am sorry. I apologised then. We drove away the

desire and terror together for a little while, did we not?"

He looked up and she was staring intently into his eyes. "Did we not?"

"We did." He took a deep breath and stretched out his hands for the goblet. "Is this some potion to sap my will and make me work for your interests?"

"No potion could do that. It will revive you, that is all."

He sipped the liquid and immediately his mouth was clean and his head clear. He drained the goblet and he felt a glow of strength in all his limbs and vitals.

"Do you still wish to die?" she asked as she received back the cup, replacing it beneath her robes.

"If death will bring me peace."

"It will not—not if you die now. That I know."

"How did you find me here?"

"Oh, by a variety of means, some of them sorcerous. But my bird brought me to you." She extended her right arm to point behind him.

He turned and there was the bird of gold and silver and brass which he himself had once ridden while in Myshella's service. Its great metallic wings were folded but there was intelligence in its emerald eyes as it waited for its mistress.

"Have you come, then, to return me to Tanelorn?"

She shook her head. "Not yet. I have come to tell you where you may discover our enemy Theleb K'aarna."

He smiled. "He threatens you again?"

"Not directly."

Elric shook sand from his cloak. "I know you well, Myshella. You would not interfere in my destiny unless it had again become in some way linked with your own. You have said that I am afraid to love you. That may be true, for I think I am afraid to love any woman. But you make use of love—the men to whom you give your love are men who will serve your purpose."

"I do not deny that. I love only heroes—and only heroes who work to ensure the presence of the Power of Law upon this plane of our Earth. . . ."

"I care not whether Law or Chaos gains predominance. Even my hatred of Theleb K'aarna has waned —and that was a personal hatred, nothing to do with any cause."

"What if you knew Theleb K'aarna once again threatens the folk of Tanelorn?"

"Impossible. Tanelorn is eternal."

"Tanelorn is eternal—but its citizens are not. I know. More than once has some catastrophe fallen upon those who dwell in Tanelorn. And the Lords of Chaos hate Tanelorn, though they cannot attack it directly. They would aid any mortal who thought he could destroy those whom the Chaos Lords regard as traitors."

Elric frowned. He knew of the enmity of the Lords of Chaos to Tanelorn. He had heard that on more than one occasion they had made use of mortals to attack the city.

"And you say Theleb K'aarna plans to destroy Tanelorn's citizens? With Chaos' aid?"

"Aye. Your thwarting of his schemes concerning Nadsokor and Rackhir's caravan made him extend his hatred to all dwelling in Tanelorn. In Troos he discovered some ancient grimoires—things which survived from the Age of the Doomed Folk."

"How can that be? They existed a whole time cycle before Melniboné!"

"True—but Troos itself has lasted since the Age of the Doomed Folk and these were people who had many great inventions, a means of preserving their wisdom. . . ."

"Very well. I will accept that Theleb K'aarna found their grimoires. What did those grimoires tell him?"

"They showed him the means of causing a rupture in the division which separates one plane of Earth from another. This knowledge of the other planes is largely mysterious to us—even your ancestors only guessed at the variety of existences obtaining in what the ancients termed the 'multiverse'—and I know only a little more than do you. The Lords of the Higher Worlds can, at times, move freely between these temporal and spatial layers, but mortals cannot—at least not in this period of our being."

"And what has Theleb K'aarna done? Surely great power would be needed to cause this 'rupture' you describe? He does not have that power."

"True. But he has powerful allies in the Chaos Lords. The Lords of Entropy have leagued themselves with him as they would league themselves with anyone who was willing to be the means of destruction of those who dwell in Tanelorn. He found more than manuscripts in the Forest of Troos. He discovered those buried devices which were the inventions of the Doomed Folk and which ultimately brought about their destruction. These devices, of course, were meaningless to him until the Lords of Chaos showed him how they could be activated using the very forces of creation for their energy."

"And he has activated them? Where?"

"He brought the device he wanted to these parts, for he needed space to work where he thought he could not be observed by such as myself."

"He is in the Sighing Desert?"

"Aye. If you had continued on your horse you would have found him by now—or he you. I believe that is what drove you into the desert—a compulsion to seek him out."

"I had no compulsion save a need to die!" Elric tried to control his anger.

She smiled again. "Have it thus if you will. . . ."

"You mean I am so manipulated by Fate that I cannot choose to die if I wish?"

"Ask yourself for that answer."

Elric's face was clouded with puzzlement and despair. "What is it, then, which guides me? And to what end?"

"You must discover that for yourself."

"You want me to go against Chaos? Yet Chaos aids me and I am sworn to Arioch."

"But you are mortal—and Arioch is slow to aid you these days, perhaps because he guesses what lies in the future."

"What do you know of the future?"

"Little—and what I know I cannot speak of to you. A mortal may choose whom he serves, Elric."

"I have chosen. I chose Chaos."

"Yet much of your melancholy is because you are divided in your loyalties."

"That, too, is true."

"Besides, you would not fight for Law if you fought against Theleb K'aarna—you would merely be fighting against one aided by Chaos—and those of Chaos often fight among themselves do they not?"

"They do. It is also well known that I hate Theleb K'aarna and would destroy him whether he served Law or Chaos."

"Therefore you will not unduly anger those to whom you are loyal—though they may be reluctant to help you."

"Tell me more of Theleb K'aarna's plans."

"You must see for yourself. There is your horse." She pointed again and this time he saw the golden mare emerge from the other side of a dune. "Head North-east as you were heading, but move cautiously lest Theleb K'aarna becomes aware of your presence and traps you."

"Suppose I merely return to Tanelorn—or choose to try to die again?"

"But you will not, will you, Elric? You have loyalties to your friends, you wish in your heart to serve what I represent—and you hate Theleb K'aarna. I do not think you would wish to die for the moment."

He scowled. "Once more I am burdened with unwanted responsibilities, hedged by considerations other than my own desires, trapped by emotions which we of

Melniboné have been taught to despise. Aye—I will
go, Myshella. I will do what you wish."

"Be careful, Elric. Theleb K'aarna now has powers
which are unfamiliar to you, which you will find difficult to combat." She gave him a lingering look and suddenly he had stepped forward and had seized her,
kissed her while tears flowed down his white face and
mingled with hers.

Later he watched as she climbed into the onyx saddle of the bird of silver and gold and called out a command. The metal wings beat with a great clashing, the
emerald eyes turned and the gem-studded beak opened.
"Farewell, Elric," said the bird.

But Myshella said nothing, did not look back.

Soon the metal bird was a speck of light in the blue
sky and Elric had turned his horse towards the North-
east.

CHAPTER THREE

The Barrier Broken

Elric reined in behind the cover of a crag. He had found the camp of Theleb K'aarna. A large tent of yellow silk had been erected beneath the protection of an overhang of rock which was part of a formation making a natural amphitheatre among the dunes of the desert. A wagon and two horses were close to the tent, but all this was dominated by the thing of metal which reared in the centre of the clearing. It was contained in an enormous bowl of clear crystal. The bowl was almost globular with a narrow opening at the top. The device itself was asymetrical and strange, composed of many curved and angular surfaces which seemed to contain myriad half-formed faces, shapes of beasts and buildings, illusive designs coming and going even as Elric looked upon it. An imagination even more grotesque than that of Elric's ancestors had fashioned the thing, amalgamating metals and other substances which logic denied could ever be fused into one thing. A creation of Chaos which offered a clue as to how the Doomed Folk had come to destroy themselves. And it was alive. Deep within it something pulsed, as delicate and tentative as the heartbeat of a dying wren. Elric had witnessed many obscenities in his life and was moved by few of them, but this device, though superficially more innocuous than much he had seen, brought bile into his mouth. Yet for all his disgust he remained where he was, fascinated by the machine in the bowl, until the flap of the yellow tent was drawn back and Theleb K'aarna emerged.

The Sorcerer of Pan Tang was paler and thinner than when Elric had last seen him, shortly before the battle between the beggars of Nadsokor and the warriors of Tanelorn. Yet unhealthy energy flushed the cheeks and burned in the dark eyes, gave a nervous swiftness to the movements. Theleb K'aarna approached the bowl.

As he came closer Elric could hear him muttering to himself.

"Now, now, now," murmured the sorcerer. "Soon, soon will die Elric and all who league with him. Ah, the albino will rue the day when he earned my vengeance and turned me from a scholar into what I am today. And when he is dead, then Queen Yishana will realise her mistake and give herself to me. How could she love that pale-faced anachronism more than a man of my great talents? How?"

Elric had almost forgotten Theleb K'aarna's obsession with Queen Yishana of Jharkor, the woman who had wielded a greater power over the sorcerer than could any magic. It had been Theleb K'aarna's jealousy of Elric which had turned him from a relatively peaceful student of the dark arts into a vengeful practitioner of the most frightful sorceries.

He watched as Theleb K'aarna began with his finger to trace complicated patterns upon the glass of the bowl. And with every completed rune the pulse within the machine grew stronger. Oddly coloured light began to flow through certain sections, bringing them to life. A steady thump issued from the neck of the bowl. A peculiar stink began to reach Elric's nostrils. The core of light became brighter and larger and the machine seemed to alter its shape, sometimes becoming apparently liquid and streaming around the inside of the bowl.

The golden mare snorted and began to shift uneasily. Elric automatically patted her neck and steadied her. Theleb K'aarna was now merely a silhouette against the swiftly changing light within the bowl. He continued to murmur to himself but his words were drowned by the heartbeats which now echoed among the surrounding rocks. His right hand drew still more invisible diagrams upon the glass.

The sky seemed to be darkening, though it was some hours to sunset. Elric looked up. Above his head the sky was still blue, the golden sun still strong, but the air around him had grown dark, as if a solitary cloud had come to cover the scene he witnessed.

Now Theleb K'aarna was stumbling back, his face stained by the strange light from the bowl, his eyes huge and mad.

"Come!" he screamed. "Come! The barrier is down!"

Elric saw a shadow then, behind the bowl. It was a shadow which dwarfed even the great machine. Something bellowed. It was scaly. It lumbered. It raised a huge and sinuous head. It reminded Elric of a dragon from one of his own caves, but it was bulkier and upon its enormous back were two rows of flapping ridges of bone. It opened its mouth to reveal row upon row of teeth and the ground shook as it walked from the other side of the bowl and stood staring down at the tiny figure of the sorcerer, its eyes stupid and angry. Another came pounding from behind the bowl, and another—great reptilian monsters from another Age of Earth. And following them came those who controlled them. The horse was snorting and prancing and desperately trying to escape, but Elric managed to calm her down again as he looked at the figures which now rested their hands on the obedient heads of the monsters. The figures were even more terrifying than the reptiles—for although they walked upon two legs and had hands of sorts they, too, were reptilian. They bore a peculiar resemblance to the dragon creatures and their size, also, was many times greater than a man's. In their hands they had ornate instruments which could only be weapons—instruments attached to their arms by spirals of golden metal. A hood of skin covered their black and green heads and red eyes glared from the shadows of their faces.

Theleb K'aarna laughed. "I have achieved it. I have

destroyed the barrier between the planes and, thanks to
the Lords of Chaos, have found allies which Elric's
sorcery cannot destroy because they do not obey the
sorcerous rules of this plane! They are invincible, invulnerable—and they obey only Theleb K'aarna!"

A huge snorting and screaming came from beasts and
warriors alike.

"Now we shall go against Tanelorn!" Theleb
K'aarna shouted. "And with this power I shall return
to Jharkor, to make fickle Yishana my own!"

Elric felt a certain sympathy for Theleb K'aarna at
that moment. Without the aid of the Lords of Chaos,
his sorcery could not have achieved this. He had given
himself up to them, had become one of their tools all
because of his weak-minded love for Jharkor's ageing
queen. Elric knew he could not go against the monsters
and their monstrous riders. He must return to Tanelorn
to warn his friends to leave the city, to hope that he
might find a means of returning these frightful inter-
lopers back to their own plane. But then the mare
screamed suddenly and reared, maddened by the sights,
the sounds and the smells she had been forced to wit-
ness. And the scream sounded in a sudden silence. The
rearing horse revealed itself to Theleb K'aarna as he
turned his mad eyes in Elric's direction.

Elric knew he could not outride the monsters. He
knew those weapons could easily destroy him from a
distance. He drew the black hellsword Stormbringer
from its scabbard and it shouted as it came free. He
drove his spurs into the horse and he rode directly
down the rocks towards the bowl while Theleb K'aarna
was still too startled to give orders to his new allies. His
one hope was that he could destroy the device—or at
least break some important part of it—and in so doing
return the monsters to their own plane.

His white face ghastly in the sorcerous darkness, his
sword raised high, he galloped past Theleb K'aarna
and struck a mighty blow at the glass protecting the
machine.

The Black Sword collided with the glass and sank

into it. Carried on by the momentum, Elric was flung from his saddle and he, too, passed through the glass without apparently breaking it. He glimpsed the dreadful planes and curves of the Doomed Folk's device. His body struck them. He felt as if the fabric of his being was disintegrating. . .

. . . and then he lay sprawled upon sweet grass and there was nothing of the desert, of Theleb K'aarna, of the pulsing machine, of the horrible beasts and their dreadful masters, only waving foliage and warm sunshine. He heard birdsong and he heard a voice.

"The storm. It has gone. And you? Are you called Elric of Melniboné?"

He picked himself up and turned. A tall man stood before him. The man was clad in a conical silver helm and was encased to the knee in a byrnie also of silver. A scarlet, longsleeved coat partly covered the byrnie. The man bore a scabbarded longsword at his side. His legs were encased in breeks of soft leather and there were boots of green-tinted doeskin on his feet. But Elric's attention was caught primarily by the man's features (which resembled those of a Melnibonéan much more than those of a true man) and the fact that he wore upon his left hand a six-fingered gauntlet encrusted with dark jewels, while over his right eye was a large patch which was also jewelled and matched the hand. The eye not covered by the patch was large and slanting and had a yellow centre and purple surrounds.

"I am Elric of Melniboné," the albino agreed. "Are you to thank for rescuing me from those creatures Theleb K'aarna summoned?"

The tall man shook his head. " 'Twas I that summoned you, but I know of no Theleb K'aarna. I was told that I had only one opportunity to receive your aid and that I must take it in this particular place at this particular time. I am called Corum Jhaelen Irsei— the Prince in the Scarlet Robe—and I ride upon a Quest of grave import."

Elric frowned. The name had a half-familiar ring, but he could not place it. He half-recalled an old dream . . .

"Where is this forest?" he asked, sheathing his sword.

"It is nowhere on your plane or in your time, Prince Elric. I summoned you to aid me in my battle against the Lords of Chaos. Already I have been instrumental in destroying two of the Sword rulers—Arioch and Xiombarg—but the third, the most powerful, remains. . . ."

"Arioch of Chaos—and Xiombarg? You have destroyed two of the most powerful members of the Company of Chaos? Yet but a month since I spoke with Arioch. He is my patron. He . . ."

"There are many planes of existence," Prince Corum told him gently. "In some the Lords of Chaos are strong. In some they are weak. In some, I have heard, they do not exist at all. You must accept that here Arioch and Xiombarg have been banished so that effectively they no longer exist in my world. It is the third of the Sword Rulers who threatens us now—the strongest, King Mabelode."

Elric frowned. "In my—plane—Mabelode is no stronger than Arioch and Xiombarg. This makes a travesty of all my understanding. . . ."

"I will explain as much as I can," said Prince Corum. "For some reason Fate has selected me to be the hero who must banish the domination of Chaos from the Fifteen Planes of Earth. I am at present travelling on my way to seek a city which we call Tanelorn, where I hope to find aid. But my guide is a prisoner in a castle close to here and before I can continue I must rescue him. I was told how I might summon aid to help me effect this rescue and I used the spell to bring you to me. I was to tell you that if you aided me, then you would aid yourself—that if I was successful then you would receive something which would make your task easier."

"Who told you this?"

"A wise man."

Elric sat down on a fallen tree-trunk, his head in his hands. "I have been drawn away at an importunate time," he said. "I pray that you speak the truth to me, Prince Corum." He looked up suddenly. "It is a marvel that you speak at all—or at least that I understand you. How can this be?"

"I was informed that we should be able to communicate easily because 'we are part of the same thing'. Do not ask me to explain more, Prince Elric, for I know no more."

Elric shrugged. "Well this may be an illusion. I may have killed myself or become digested by that machine of Theleb K'aarna's, but plainly I have no choice but to agree to aid you in the hope that I am, in turn, aided."

Prince Corum left the clearing and returned with two horses, one white and one black. He offered the reins of the black horse to Elric.

Elric settled himself in the unfamiliar saddle. "You spoke of Tanelorn. It is for the sake of Tanelorn that I find myself in this dreamworld of yours."

Prince Corum's face was eager. "You know where Tanelorn lies?"

"In my own world, aye—but why should it lie in this one?"

"Tanelorn lies in all planes, though in different guises. There is one Tanelorn and it is eternal with many forms."

They were riding through the gentle forest along a narrow track.

Elric accepted what Corum said. There was a dreamlike quality about his presence here and he decided that he must regard all events here as he would regard the events in a dream. "Where go we now?" he asked casually. "To the castle?"

Corum shook his head. "First we must have the Third Hero—the Many-named Hero."

"And will you summon him with sorcery, too?"

"I was told not. I was told that he would meet us—

drawn from whichever Age he exists in by the necessity to complete the Three Who Are One."

"And what mean these phrases? What is the Three Who Are One?"

"I know little more than you, friend Elric, save that it will need all three of us to defeat him who holds my guide prisoner."

"Aye," murmured Elric feelingly, "and it will need more than that to save my Tanelorn from Theleb K'aarna's reptiles. Even now they must march against the city."

CHAPTER FOUR

The Vanishing Tower.

The road widened and left the forest to
wander among the heather of high and hilly moorland
country. Far away to the west they could see cliffs,
and beyond the cliffs was the deeper blue of the
ocean. A few birds circled in the wide sky. It seemed
a particularly peaceful world and Elric could hardly
believe that it was under attack from the forces of
Chaos. As they rode Corum explained that his gauntlet was not a gauntlet at all, but the hand of an alien
being, grafted on to his arm, just as his eye was an
alien eye which could see into a terrifying netherworld from which Corum could bring aid if he chose
to do so.

"All you tell me makes the complicated sorceries
and cosmologies of my world seem simple in com-
parison," Elric smiled as they crossed the peaceful
landscape.

"It only seems complicated because it is strange,"
Corum said. "Your world would doubtless seem in-
comprehensible to me if I were suddenly flung into it.
Besides," he laughed, "this particular plane is not my
world, either, though it resembles it more than do
many. We have one thing in common, Elric, and that
is that we are both doomed to play a role in the constant struggle between the Lords of the Higher
Worlds—and we shall never understand why that
struggle takes place, why it is eternal. We fight, we
suffer agonies of mind and soul, but we are never sure
that our suffering is worthwhile."

"You are right," Elric said feelingly. "We have much in common, you and I, Corum."

Corum was about to reply when he saw something on the road ahead. It was a mounted warrior. He sat perfectly still as if he awaited them. "Perhaps this is the Third of whom Bolorhiag spoke."

Cautiously, they rode forward.

The man they approached stared at them from a brooding face. He was as tall as them, but bulkier. His skin was jet black and he wore upon his head and shoulders the stuffed head and pelt of a snarling bear. His plate armour was also black, without insignia, and at his side was a great black-hilted sword in a black scabbard. He rode a massive roan stallion and there was a heavy round shield attached to the back of his saddle. As Elric and Corum came closer the man's handsome negroid features assumed an astonished expression and he gasped.

"I know you! I know you both!"

Elric, too, felt he recognised the man, just as he had noticed something familiar in Corum's features.

"How came you here to Balwyn Moor, friend?" Corum asked him.

The man looked about him as if in a daze. "Balwyn Moor? This is Balwyn Moor? I have been here but a few moments. Before that I was—I was . . . Ah! The memory starts to fade again." He pressed a large hand to his forehead. "A name—another name! No more! Elric! Corum! But I—I am now . . ."

"How do you know our names?" Elric asked him. A mood of dread had seized the albino. He felt that he should not ask these questions, that he should not know the answers.

"Because—don't you see?—I am Elric—I am Corum—oh, this is the worst agony. . . . Or, at least, I have been or am to be Elric or Corum. . . ."

"Your name, sir?" Corum said again.

"A thousand names are mine. A thousand heroes I have been. Ah! I am—I am—John Daker—Erekosë —Urlik—many, many, many, more. . . . The memories, the dreams, the existences." He stared at them suddenly through his pain-filled eyes. "Do you not understand? Am I the only one to be doomed to understand? I am he who has been called the Champion Eternal—I am the hero who has existed forever —and, yes, I am Elric of Melniboné—Prince Corum Jhaelen Irsei—I am you, also. We three are the same creature and a myriad other creatures besides. We three are one thing—doomed to struggle forever and never understand why. Oh! My head pounds. Who tortures me so? Who?

Elric's throat was dry. "You say you are another incarnations of *myself!*"

"If you would phrase it so! You are both other incarnations of *myself!*"

"So," said Corum, "that is what Bolorhiag meant by the Three Who Are One. We are all aspects of the same man, yet we have trippled our strength because we have been drawn from three different ages. It is the only power which might successfully go against Voilodion Ghagnasdiak of the Vanishing Tower."

"Is that the castle wherein your guide is imprisoned?" Elric asked, casting a glance of sympathy at the groaning black man.

"Aye. The Vanishing Tower flickers from one plane to another, from one age to another, and exists in a single location only for a few moments at a time. But because we are three separate incarnations of a single hero it is possible that we form a sorcery of some kind which will enable us to follow the tower and attack it. Then, if we free my guide, we can continue on to Tanelorn. . . ."

"Tanelorn?" The black man looked at Corum with hope suddenly flooding into his eyes. "I, too, seek Tanelorn. Only there may I discover some remedy to my dreadful fate—which is to know all previous incarnations and be hurled at random from one existence to another! Tanelorn—I must find her!"

"I, too, must discover Tanelorn," Elric told him,

"for on my own plane her inhabitants are in great danger."

"So we have a common purpose as well as a common identity," Corum said. "Therefore we shall fight in concert, I pray. First we must free my guide, then go on to Tanelorn."

"I'll aid you willingly," said the black giant.

"And what shall we call you—you who are ourselves?" Corum asked him.

"Call me Erekosë—though another name suggests itself to me—for it was as Erekosë that I came closest to knowing forgetfulness and the fulfilment of love."

"Then you are to be envied, Erekosë," Elric said meaningly, "for at least you have come close to forgetfulness. . . ."

"You have no inkling of what it is I must forget," the black giant told him. He shook his reins. "Now Corum—which way to the Vanishing Tower?"

"This road leads to it. We ride down now to Darkvale, I believe."

Elric's mind could hardly contain the significance of what he had heard. It suggested that the universe—or the multiverse, as Myshella had named it—was divided into infinite layers of existence, that time was virtually a meaningless concept save where it related to one man's life or one short period of history. And there were planes of existence where the Cosmic Balance was not known at all—or so Corum had suggested—and other planes where the Lords of the Higher Worlds had far greater powers than they had on his own world. He was tempted to consider the idea of forgetting Theleb K'aarna, Myshella, Tanelorn and the rest and devote himself to the exploration of all these infinite worlds. But then he knew that this could not be for, if Erekosë spoke the truth, then he—or something which was essentially himself—existed in all these planes already. Whatever force it was which he named "Fate" had admitted him to this plane to fulfil one purpose. An important purpose affecting the destinies of a thousand planes it must surely be if it brought him together in three separate incarnations. He glanced curiously at the black giant on his left, at the maimed man with the jewelled hand and eye on his right. Were they really himself?

Now he fancied he felt some of the desperation Erekosë must feel—to remember all those other incarnations, all those other mistakes, all that other pointless conflict—and never to know the purpose for it all, if purpose indeed there were.

"Darkvale," said Corum pointing down the hill.

The road ran steeply until it passed between two looming cliffs, disappearing in shadow. There was something particularly gloomy about the place.

"I am told there was a village here once," Corum said to them. "An uninviting spot, eh, brothers?"

"I have seen worse," murmured Erekosë. "Come, let's get all this done with. . . ." He spurred his roan ahead of the others and galloped at great speed down the steep path. They followed his example and soon they had passed between the lowering cliffs and could barely see ahead of them as they continued to follow the road through the shadows.

And now Elric saw ruins huddled close to the foot of the cliffs on either side. Oddly twisted ruins which had not been the result of age or warfare—these ruins were warped, fused, as if Chaos had touched them while passing through the vale.

Corum had been studying the ruins carefully and at length he reined in. "There," he said. "That pit. Here is where we must wait."

Elric looked at the pit. It was ragged and deep and the earth in it seemed freshly turned as if it had been but lately dug. "What must we wait for, Friend Corum?"

"For the Tower," said Prince Corum. "I would guess that this is where it appears when it is in this plane."

"And when will it appear?"

"At no particular time. We must wait. And then, as soon as we see it, we must rush it and attempt to enter before it vanishes again, moving on to the next plane."

Erekosë's face was impassive. He dismounted and sat on the hard ground with his back against a slab of rock which had once belonged to a house.

"You seem more patient than I, Erekosë," said Elric.

"I have learned patience, for I have lived since time began and will live on at the end of time."

Elric got down from his own black horse and loosened its girth strap while Corum prowled about the edge of the pit. "Who told you that the Tower would appear here?" Elric asked him.

"A sorcerer who doubtless serves Law as I do, for I am a mortal doomed to battle Chaos."

"As am I," said Erekosë the Champion Eternal.

"As am I," said Elric of Melnibonë, "though I am sworn to serve it."

Elric looked at his two companions and it was possible to believe that these were two incarnations of himself. Certainly their lives, their struggles, their personalities, to some extent, were very similar.

"And why do you seek Tanelorn, Erekosë?" he asked.

"I have been told that I may find peace there— and wisdom—a means of returning to the world of the Eldren where dwells the woman I love, for it has been said that since Tanelorn exists in all planes at all times it is easier for a man who dwells there to pass between the planes, discover the particular one he seeks. What interest have you in Tanelorn, Lord Elric?"

"I know Tanelorn and I know that you are right to seek it. My mission seems to be the defence of that city upon my own plane—but even now my friends may be destroyed by that which has been brought against them. I pray Corum is right and that in the

Vanishing Tower I shall find a means to defeat Theleb K'aarna's beasts and their masters."

Corum raised his jewelled hand to his jewelled eye. "I seek Tanelorn for I have heard the city can aid me in my struggle against Chaos."

"But Tanelorn will fight neither Law nor Chaos— that is why she exists for eternity," Elric said.

"Aye. Like Erekosë I do not seek swords but wisdom."

Night fell and Darkvale grew gloomier. While the others watched the pit Elric tried to sleep, but his fears for Tanelorn were too great. Would Myshella try to defend the city? Would Moonglum and Rackhir die? And what could he possibly find in the Vanishing Tower which would aid him? He heard the murmuring of conversation as his other selves discussed how Darkvale had come to exist.

"I heard that Chaos once attacked the town which at that time lay in a quiet valley," Corum told Erekosë. "The tower was then the property of a knight who gave shelter to one whom Chaos hated. They brought a huge force of creatures against Darkvale, raising and compressing the walls of the valley, but the knight sought the aid of Law who enabled him to shift his tower into another dimension. Then Chaos decreed that the tower should shift forever, never being on one plane longer than a few hours, usually for never more than a few moments. The knight and the fugitive went mad at last and killed each other. Then Voilodion Ghagnasdiak found the tower and became resident therein. Too late he realised his mistake as he was shifted from his own plane to an alien one. Since then he has been too fearful to leave the tower but desperate for company. He has taken to the habit of capturing whomever he can and forcing them to be his companions in the Vanishing Tower until they bore him. When they bore him, he slays them."

"And your guide may soon be slain? What manner of creature is this Voilodion Ghagnasdiak?"

"He is a monstrous evil creature commanding great powers of destruction, that is all I know."

"Which is why the gods have seen fit to call up three aspects of myself to attack the Vanishing Tower," said Erekosë. "It must be important to them."

"It is to me," said Corum, "for the guide is also my friend and the very existence of the Fifteen Planes is threatened if I cannot find Tanelorn soon."

Elric heard Erekosë laugh bitterly. "Why cannot I—we—ever be faced with a small problem, a domestic problem. Why are we forever involved with the destiny of the universe?"

Corum replied just as Elric began to nod into a half-doze. "Perhaps domestic problems are worse. Who knows?"

CHAPTER FIVE

Jhary-a-Conel

        "It is here! Hasten Elric!"

Elric sprang up.

It was dawn. He had already stood watch once during the night.

He drew his Black Sword from its scabbard noticing with some astonishment that Erekosë had already drawn his own blade and that it was almost identical to his own.

There was the Vanishing Tower.

Corum was running towards it even now.

The tower was in fact a small castle of grey and solid stone, but about its battlements played lights and its outline was not altogether clear at certain sections of its walls.

Elric ran beside Erekosë.

"He keeps the door open to lure his 'guests' in," panted the black giant. "It is our only advantage, I think."

The tower flickered.

"Hasten!" Corum cried again and the Prince in the Scarlet Robe dashed into the darkness of the doorway.

"Hasten!"

They ran into a small antechamber which was lit by a great oil lamp hanging from the ceiling by chains.

The door closed suddenly behind them.

Elric glanced at Erekosë's tense black features, at Corum's blemished face. All had swords ready, but now a profound silence filled the hall. Without speaking Corum pointed through a window-slit. The view beyond it had changed. They seemed now to be looking out over blue sea.

"Jhary!" Corum called. "Jhary-a-Conel!"

A faint sound came back. It might have been a reply or it might have been the squeak of a rat in the castle walls. "Jhary!" Corum cried again. "Voilodion Ghagnasdiak? Am I to be thwarted? Have you left this place?"

"I have not left it. What do you want with me?" The voice came from the next room. Warily the three heroes who were one hero went forward.

Something like lightning flickered in the room and in its ghastly glare Elric saw Voilodion Ghagnasdiak.

He was a dwarf clad all in puffed multicoloured silks, furs and satins, a tiny sword in his hand. His head was too large for his body, but it was a handsome head with thick black eyebrows which met in the middle. He smiled at them. "At last someone new to relieve my ennui. But lay down your swords, gentlemen, I beg you, for you are to be my guests."

"I know what fate your guests may expect," Corum said. "Know this, Voilodion Ghagnasdiak, we have come to release Jhary-a-Conel whom you hold prisoner. Give him up to us and we will not harm you."

The dwarf's handsome features grinned cheerfully at these words. "But I am very powerful. You cannot defeat me. Watch."

He waved his sword and more lightning lashed about the room. Elric half-raised his sword to ward it off, but it never quite touched him. He stepped angrily towards the dwarf. "Know this, Voilodion Ghagnasdiak, I am Elric of Melniboné and I have much power. I bear the Black Sword and it thirsts to drink your soul unless you release Prince Corum's friend!"

Again the dwarf laughed. "Swords? What power have they?"

"Our swords are not ordinary blades," Erekosë said. "And we have been brought here by forces you could not comprehend—wrenched from our own ages by the power of the gods themselves—specifically to demand that this Jhary-a-Conel be given up to us."

"You are deceived," said Voilodion Ghagnasdiak, "or you seek to deceive me. This Jhary is a witty fellow, I'd agree, but what interest could gods have in him?"

Elric raised Stormbringer. The Black Sword moaned in anticipation of a quenching.

Then the dwarf produced a tiny yellow ball from nowhere and flung it at Elric. It bounced on his forehead and he was flung backward across the room, Stormbringer clattering from his hand. Dizzily Elric tried to rise, reached out to take his sword, but he was too weak. On impulse he began to cry for the aid of Arioch, but then he remembered that Arioch had been banished from this world. There were no supernatural allies to call upon here—none but the sword and he could not reach the sword.

Erekosë leapt backward and kicked the Black Sword in Elric's direction. As the albino's hand encircled the hilt he felt strength come back to him, but it was no more than ordinary mortal strength. He climbed to his feet.

Corum remained where he was. The dwarf was still laughing. Another ball appeared in his hand. Again he flung it at Elric, but this time he brought up the Black Sword in time and deflected it. It bounced across the room and exploded against the far wall. Something black writhed from the fire.

"It is dangerous to destroy the globes," said Voilodion Ghagnasdiak equably, "for now what is in them will destroy you."

The black thing grew. The flames died.

"I am free," said a voice.

"Aye." Voilodion Ghagnasdiak was gleeful. "Free to kill these fools who reject my hospitality!"

"Free to be slain," Elric replied as he watched the thing take shape.

At first it seemed all made of flowing hair which gradually compressed until it formed the outline of a creature with the heavily muscled body of a gorilla, though the hide was thick and warted like that of a rhinoceros. From behind the shoulders curved great black wings and on the neck was the snarling head of a tiger. It clutched a long, scythe-like weapon in its hairy hands. The tiger head roared and the scythe swept out suddenly, barely missing Elric.

Erekosë and Corum began to move forward to Elric's aid. Elric heard Corum cry: "My eye—it will not see into the netherworld. I cannot summon help!" It seemed that Corum's sorcerous powers were also limited on this plane. Then Voilodion Ghagnasdiak threw a yellow ball at the black giant and the pale man with the jewelled hand. Both barely managed to deflect the missiles and, in so doing, caused them to burst. Immediately shapes emerged and became two more of the winged tiger-men and Elric's allies were forced to defend themselves.

As he dodged another swing of the scythe Elric tried to think of some rune which would summon supernatural aid to him, but he could think of none which would work here. He thrust at the tiger-man but his blow was blocked by the scythe. His opponent was enormously strong and swift. The black wings began to beat and the snarling thing flapped upwards to the ceiling, hovered for a moment and then rushed down on Elric with its scythe whirling, a chilling scream coming from its fanged mouth, its yellow eyes glaring.

Elric felt something close to panic. Stormbringer was not supplying him with the strength he expected. Its powers were diminished on this plane. He barely managed to dodge the scythe again and lash at the creature's exposed thigh. The blade bit but no blood came. The tiger-man did not seem to notice the wound. Again it began to flap towards the ceiling.

Elric saw that his companions were experiencing a similar plight. Corum's face was full of consternation as if he had expected an easy victory and now foresaw defeat.

Meanwhile Voilodion Ghagnasdiak continued to scream his glee and flung more of the yellow balls about the room. As each one burst there emerged another snarling winged tiger creature. The room was full of them. Elric, Erekosë and Corum backed to the far wall as the monsters bore down on them, their ears full of the fearful beating of the giant wings, the harsh screams of hatred.

"I fear I have summoned you two to your destruction," Corum panted. "I had no warning that our powers would be so limited here. The tower must shift so fast that even the ordinary laws of sorcery do not apply within its walls."

"They seem to work well enough for the dwarf," Elric said as he brought up his blade to block first one scythe and then another. "If I could slay but a single . . ."

His back was hard against the wall, a scythe nicked his cheek and drew blood, another tore his cloak, another slashed his arm. The tiger faces were grinning now as they closed in.

Elric aimed a blow at the head of the nearest creature, struck off its ear so that it howled. Stormbringer howled back and stabbed at the thing's throat.

But the sword hardly penetrated and served only to put the tiger-man slightly off balance.

As the thing staggered Elric wrenched the scythe from its hands and reversed the weapon, drawing the blade across the chest. The tiger-man screamed as blood spurted from the wound.

"I was right!" Elric shouted at the others. "Only their own weapons can harm them!" He moved forward with the scythe in one hand and Stormbringer in the other. The tiger-men backed off and then began to flap upwards to hover near the ceiling.

Elric ran towards Voilodion Ghagnasdiak. The dwarf gave a yell of terror and disappeared through a doorway too small easily to admit Elric.

Then, with thundering wings, the tiger creatures descended again.

This time the other two strove to capture scythes from their enemies. Driving back those who attacked

him, the albino prince took Corum's main assailant
from behind and the thing fell with its head sliced off.
Corum sheathed his longsword and plucked up the
scythe, killing a third tiger-man almost immediately and
kicking the fallen scythe towards Erekosë. Black feathers drifted in the stinking air. The flagstones of the
floor were slippery with blood. The three heroes drove
a path through their enemies into the smaller room they
had lately left. Still the tiger creatures came on, but
now they had to pass through the door and this was
more easily defended.

Glancing back Elric saw the window slit of the
tower. Outside the scenery altered constantly as the
Vanishing Tower continued its erratic progress through
the planes of existence. But the three were wearying
and all had lost some blood from minor wounds.
Scythes clashed on scythes as the fight continued,
wings beat loudly and the snarling faces spat at them
and spoke words which could barely be understood.
Without the strength supplied him by his hell-forged
sword Elric was weakening rapidly. Twice he staggered
and was borne up by the others. Was he to die in some
alien world with his friends never knowing how he had
perished? But then he remembered that his friends
were even now under attack from the reptilian beasts
Theleb K'aarna had sent against Tanelorn, that they,
too, would soon be dead. This knowledge gave him a
little more strength and enabled him to sweep his
scythe deep into the belly of another tiger creature.

This gap in the ranks of the sorcerous things enabled
him to see the small doorway on the far side of the
other room. Voilodion Ghagnasdiak was crouched
there, hurling still more of the yellow globes. New
winged tiger-men grew up to replace those who had
fallen.

But then Elric heard Voilodion Ghagnasdiak give a
yell and saw that something was covering his face. It
was a black and white animal with small black wings
which beat in the air. Some offspring of the beasts who
attacked him? Elric could not tell. But Voilodion Ghag-

nasdiak was plainly terrified of it, trying to drag it from his face.

Another figure appeared behind the dwarf. Bright eyes peered from an intelligent face framed by long black hair. He was dressed as ostentatiously as the dwarf, but he was unarmed. He was calling to Elric and the albino strained to catch the words even as another tiger-creature came at him.

Corum saw the newcomer now. "Jhary!" he shouted.

"The one you came to save?" Elric asked.

"Aye."

Elric made to press forward into the room, but Jhary-a-Conel waved him back. "No! No! Stay there!"

Elric frowned, was about to ask why when he was attacked from two sides by the tiger creatures and had to retreat, slashing his scythe this way and that.

"Link arms!" Jhary-a-Conel cried. "Corum in the centre—and you two draw your swords!"

Elric was panting. He slew another tiger-man and felt a new pain shoot through his leg. Blood gushed from his calf.

Voilodion Ghagnasdiak was still struggling with the thing which clung to his face.

"Hurry!" cried Jhary-a-Conel. "It is your only chance—and mine!"

Elric looked at Corum.

"He is wise, my friend," Corum said. "He knows many things which we do not. Here, I will stand in the centre."

Erekosë linked his brawny arm with Corum's and Elric did the same on the other side. Erekosë drew his sword in his left hand and Elric brought forth Stormbringer in his right.

And something began to happen. A sense of energy came back, then a sense of great physical well-being. Elric looked at his companions and laughed. It was almost as if by combining their powers they had made them four times stronger—as if they had become one entity.

A peculiar feeling of euphoria filled Elric and he

knew that Erekosë had spoken the truth—that they were three aspects of the same being.

"Let us finish them!" he shouted—and he saw that they shouted the same. Laughing the linked three strode into the chamber and now the two swords wounded whenever they struck, slaying swiftly and bringing them more energy still.

The winged tiger-men became frantic, flapping about the room as the Three Who Were One pursued them. All three were drenched in their own blood and that of their enemies, all three were laughing, invulnerable, acting completely in unison.

And as they moved the room itself began to shake. They heard Voilodion Ghagnasdiak screaming.

"The tower! The tower! This will destroy the tower!"

Elric looked up from the last corpse. It was true that the tower was swaying wildly from side to side like a ship in a storm.

Jhary-a-Conel pushed past the dwarf and entered the room of death. The sight seemed obnoxious to him but he controlled his feelings. "It is true. The sorcery we have worked today must have its effect. Whiskers—to me!"

The thing on Voilodion Ghagnasdiak's face flew into the air and settled on Jhary's shoulder. Elric saw that it was a small black and white cat, ordinary in every detail save for its neat pair of wings which it was now folding.

Voilodion Ghagnasdiak sat crumpled in the doorway and he was weeping through sightless eyes. Tears of blood flowed down his handsome face.

Elric ran back into the other room, breaking his link with Corum. He peered through the window slit. But now there was nothing but a wild eruption of mauve and purple cloud.

He gasped. "We are in limbo!"

Silence fell. Still the tower swayed. The lights were extinguished by a strange wind blowing through the rooms and the only illumination came from outside where the mist still swirled.

Jhary-a-Conel was frowning to himself as he joined Elric at the window.

"How did you know what to do?" Elric asked him.

"I knew because I know you, Elric of Melniboné— just as I know Erekosë there—for I travel in many ages and on many planes. That is why I am sometimes called Companion to Champions. I must find my sword and my sack—also my hat. Doubtless all are in Voilodion's vault with his other loot."

"But the tower? If it is destroyed shall we, too, be destroyed?"

"A possibility. Come, friend Elric, help me seek my hat."

"At such a time, you look for a—hat?"

"Aye." Jhary-a-Conel returned to the larger room, stroking the black and white cat. Voilodion Ghagnas-diak was still there and he was still weeping. "Prince Corum—Lord Erekosë—will you come with me, too."

Corum and the black giant joined Elric and they squeezed into the narrow passage, inching their way along until it widened to reveal a flight of stairs leading downward. The tower shuddered again. Jhary lit a brand and removed it from its place in the wall. He began to descend the steps, the three heroes behind him.

A slab of masonry fell from the roof and crashed just in front of Elric. "I would prefer to seek a means of escape from the tower," he said to Jhary-a-Conel. "If it falls now, we shall be buried."

"Trust me, Prince Elric," was all that Jhary would say.

And because Jhary had already shown himself to possess great knowledge Elric allowed the dandy to lead him further into the bowels of the tower.

At last they reached a circular chamber and in it was set a huge metal door.

"Voilodion's vault," Jhary told them. "Here you will find all the things you seek. And I, I hope, will find my hat. The hat was specially made and is the only one which properly matches my other clothes. . . ."

"How do we open a door like that?" Erekosë asked. "It is made of steel, surely!" He hefted the black blade he still bore in his left hand.

"If you link arms again, my friends," Jhary suggested with a kind of mocking deference, "I will show you how the door may be opened."

Once again Elric, Corum and Erekosë linked their arms together. Once again the supernatural strength seemed to flow through them and they laughed at each other, knowing that they were all part of the same creature.

Jhary's voice seemed to come faintly to Elric's ears. "And now, Prince Corum, if you would strike with your foot once upon the door. . . ."

They moved until they were close to the door. That part of them which was Corum struck out with his foot at the slab of steel—and the door fell inward as if made of the lightest wood.

This time Elric was much more reluctant to break the link which held them. But he did so at last as Jhary stepped into the vault chuckling to himself.

The tower lurched. All three were flung after Jhary into Voilodion's vault. Elric fell heavily against a great golden chair of a kind he had once seen used as an elephant saddle. He looked around the vault. It was full of valuables, of clothes, shoes, weapons. He felt nauseated as he realised that these had been the possessions of all those Voilodion had chosen to call his guests.

Jhary pulled a bundle from under a pile of furs. "Look, Prince Elric. These are what you will need where Tanelorn is concerned." It seemed to be a bunch of long sticks rolled in thin sheets of metal.

Elric accepted the heavy bundle. "What is it?"

"They are the banners of bronze and the arrows of quartz. Useful weapons against the reptilian men of Pio and their mounts."

"You know of those reptiles? You know of Theleb K'aarna, too?"

"The sorcerer of Pan Tang? Aye."

Elric stared almost suspiciously at Jhary-a-Conel. "How can you know all this?"

"I have told you. I have lived many lives as a Friend of Heroes. Unwrap this bundle when you return to Tanelorn. Use the arrows of quartz like spears. To use the banners of bronze, merely unfurl them. Aha!" Jhary reached behind a sack of jewels and came up with a somewhat dusty hat. He smacked off the dust and placed it on his head. "Ah!" He bent again and displayed a goblet. He offered this to Prince Corum. "Take it. It will prove useful, I think."

From another corner Jhary took a small sack and put it on his shoulder. Almost as an afterthought he hunted about in a chest of jewels and found a gleaming ring of unnamable stones and peculiar metal. "This is your reward, Erekosë, in helping to free me from my captor."

Erekosë smiled. "I have the feeling you needed no help, young man."

"You are mistaken, friend Erekosë. I doubt if I have ever been in greater peril." He looked vaguely about the vault, staggering as the floor tilted alarmingly.

Elric said: "We should take steps to leave."

"Exactly." Jhary-a-Conel crossed swiftly to the far side of the vault. "The last thing. In his pride Voilodion showed me his possessions, but he did not know the value of all of them."

"What do you mean?" asked the Prince in the Scarlet Robe.

"He killed the traveller who brought this with him. The traveller was right in assuming he had the means to stop the tower from vanishing, but he did not have time to use it before Voilodion had slain him." Jhary picked up a small staff coloured a dull ochre. "Here it is. The Runestaff. Hawkmoon had this with him when I travelled with him to the Dark Empire. . . ."

Noticing their puzzlement, Jhary-a-Conel, Compan-

ion to Champions, apologised. "I am sorry. I sometimes forget that not all of us have memories of other
careers. . . ."

"What is the Runestaff?" Corum asked.

"I remember one description—but I am poor at
naming and explaining things. . . ."

"That has not escaped my notice," Elric said, almost smiling.

"It is an object which can only exist under a certain
set of spacial and temporal laws. In order to continue to
exist, it must exert a field in which it can contain itself.
That field must accord with those laws—the same laws
under which we best survive."

More masonry fell.

"The tower is breaking up!" Erekosë growled.

Jhary stroked the dull ochre staff. "Please gather
near me, my friends."

The three heroes stood around him. And then the
roof of the tower fell in. But it did not fall on them for
they stood suddenly on firm ground breathing fresh air.
But there was blackness all around them. "Do not step
outside this small area," Jhary warned, "or you will be
doomed. Let the Runestaff seek what we seek."

They saw the ground change colour, breathed
warmer, then colder, air. It was as if they moved from
plane to plane of the universe, never seeing more than
the few feet of ground upon which they stood.

And then there was harsh desert sand beneath their
feet and Jhary shouted. "Now!" The four of them
rushed out of the area and into the blackness to find
themselves suddenly in sunlight beneath a sky like
beaten metal.

"A desert," Erekosë murmured. "A vast desert. . . ."

Jhary smiled. "Do you not recognise it, friend Elric?"

"Is it the Sighing Desert?"

"Listen."

And sure enough Elric heard the familiar sound of
the wind as it made its mournful passage across the
sands. A little way away he saw the Runestaff where
they had left it. Then it was gone.

"Are you all to come with me to the defence of Tanelorn?" he asked Jhary.

Jhary shook his head. "No. We go the other way. We go to seek the device Theleb K'aarna activated with the help of the Lords of Chaos. Where lies it?"

Elric tried to get his bearings. He lifted a hesitant finger. "That way, I think."

"Then let us go to it now."

"But I must try to help Tanelorn."

"You must destroy the device after we have used it, friend Elric, lest Theleb K'aarna or his like try to activate it again."

"But Tanelorn . . ."

"I do not believe that Theleb K'aarna and his beasts have yet reached the city."

"Not reached it! So much time has passed!"

"Less than a day."

Elric rubbed at his face. He said reluctantly: "Very well. I will take you to the machine."

"But if Tanelorn lies so near," Corum said to Jhary, "why seek it elsewhere?"

"Because this is not the Tanelorn we wish to find," Jhary told him.

"It will suit me," Erekosë said. "I will remain with Elric. Then, perhaps . . ."

A look almost of terror spread over Jhary's features then. He said sadly: "My friend—already much of time and space is threatened with destruction. Eternal barriers could soon fall—the fabric of the multiverse could decay. You do not understand. Such a thing as has happened in the Vanishing Tower can only happen once or twice in an eternity and even then it is dangerous to all concerned. You must do as I say. I promise that you will have just as good a chance of finding Tanelorn where I take you. Your opportunity lies in Elric's future."

Erekosë bowed his head. "Very well."

"Come," Elric said impatiently, beginning to strike off to the North-east. "For all your talk of Time, there is precious little left for me."

CHAPTER SIX

Pale Lord Shouting in Sunlight

The machine in the bowl was where Elric had last seen it, just before he had attacked it and found himself plunged into Corum's world.

Jhary seemed completely familiar with it and soon had its heart beating strongly. He shepherded the other two up to it and made them stand with their backs against the crystal. Then he handed something to Elric. It was a small vial.

"When we have departed," he said, "hurl this through the top of the bowl, then take your horse which I see is yonder and ride as fast as you can for Tanelorn. Follow these instructions perfectly and you will serve us all."

Elric accepted the vial. "Very well."

"And," Jhary said finally as he took his place with the others, "please give my compliments to my brother Moonglum."

"You know him? What—?"

"Farewell, Elric! We shall doubtless meet many times in the future, though we may not recognise each other."

Then the beating of the thing in the bowl grew louder and the ground shook and the strange darkness surrounded it—then the three figures had gone. Swiftly Elric hurled the vial upwards so that it fell through the opening of the bowl, then he ran to where his golden mare was tethered, leapt into the saddle with the bundle Jhary had given him under his arm, and galloped as fast as he could go towards Tanelorn.

Behind him the beating suddenly ceased. The dark-

168

ness disappeared. A tense silence fell. Then Elric heard something like a giant's gasp and blinding blue light filled the desert. He looked back. Not only the bowl and the device had gone—so also had the rocks which had once surrounded it.

He came up behind them at last, just before they reached the walls of Tanelorn. Elric saw warriors on those walls.

The massive reptilian monsters bore their equally repulsive masters upon their backs, their feet leaving deep marks in the sand as they moved. And Theleb K'aarna rode at their head on a chestnut stallion—and there was something draped across his saddle.

Then a shadow passed over Elric's head and he looked up. It was the metal bird which had borne Myshella away. But it was riderless. It wheeled over the heads of the lumbering reptiles whose masters raised their strange weapons and sent hissing streams of fire in its direction, driving it higher into the sky. Why was the bird here and not Myshella? A peculiar cry came again and again from its metal throat and Elric realised what that cry resembled—the pathetic sound of a mother bird whose young is in danger.

He stared hard at the bundle over Theleb K'aarna's saddle and suddenly he knew what it must be. Myshella herself! Doubtless she had given Elric up for dead and had tried to go against Theleb K'aarna only to be beaten.

Anger boiled in the albino. All his intense hatred for the sorcerer revived and his hand went to his sword. But then he looked again at the vulnerable walls of Tanelorn, at his brave companions on the battlements, and he knew that his first duty was to help them.

But how was he to reach the walls without Theleb K'aarna seeing him and destroying him before he could bring the banners of bronze to his friends? He prepared to spur his horse forward and hope that he would be lucky. Then a shadow passed over his head again and he saw that it was the metal bird flying low, something

like agony in its emerald eyes. He heard its voice.
"Prince Elric! We must save her."

He shook his head as the bird settled in the sand.
"First I must save Tanelorn."

"I will help you," said the bird of gold and silver and
brass. "Climb up into my saddle."

Elric cast a glance towards the distant monsters.
Their attention was now wholly upon the city they intended to destroy. He jumped from his horse and
crossed the sand to clamber into the onyx saddle of the
bird. The wings began to clash and with a rush they
swept into the sky, turning towards Tanelorn.

More streaks of fire hissed around them as they
neared the city, but the bird flew rapidly from side to
side and avoided them. Down they drifted now to the
gentle city, to land on the wall itself.

"Elric!" Moonglum came running along the defences.
"We were told you were dead!"

"By whom?"

"By Myshella and by Theleb K'aarna when he de-
manded our surrender."

"I suppose they could only believe that," Elric said,
separating the staffs around which were furled the thin
sheets of bronze. "Here, you must take these. I am told
that they will be useful against the reptiles of Pio. Unfurl them along the walls. Greetings, Rackhir." He
handed the astounded Red Archer one of the banners.

"You do not stay to fight with us?" Rackhir asked.

Elric looked down at the twelve slender arrows in
his hand. Each one was perfectly carved from multicoloured quartz so that even the fletchings seemed like
real feathers. "No," he said. "I hope to rescue Myshella
from Theleb K'aarna—and I can use these arrows
better from the air, also."

"Myshella, thinking you dead, seemed to go mad,"
Rackhir told him. "She conjured up various sorceries
against Theleb K'aarna—but he retaliated. At last she
flung herself from the saddle of that bird you ride—
flung herself upon him armed only with a knife. But he
overpowered her and has threatened to slay her if we

do not allow ourselves to be killed without retaliating. I know that he will kill Myshella anyway. I have been in something of a quandary of conscience. . . ."

"I will resolve that quandary, I hope." Elric stroked the metallic neck of the bird. "Come, my friend, into the air again. Remember, Rackhir—unfurl the banners along the walls as soon as I have gained a good height."

The Red Archer nodded, his face puzzled, and once again Elric was rising into the air, the arrows of quartz clutched in his left hand.

He heard Theleb K'aarna's laughter from below. He saw the monstrous beasts moving inexorably towards the walls. The gates opened suddenly and a group of horsemen rode out. Plainly they had hoped to sacrifice themselves in order to save Tanelorn and Rackhir had not had time to warn them of Elric's message.

The riders galloped wildly towards the reptilian monsters of Pio, their swords and lances waving, their yells rising to where Elric drifted high above. The monsters roared and opened their huge jaws, their masters pointed their ornate weapons at the horsemen of Tanelorn. Flames burst from the muzzles, the riders shrieked as they were devoured by the dazzling heat.

In horror Elric directed the metal bird downwards. And at last Theleb K'aarna saw him and reined in his horse, his eyes wide with fear and rage. "You are dead! You are dead!"

The great wings beat at the air as the bird hovered over Theleb K'aarna's head. "I am alive, Theleb K'aarna—and I come to destroy you at long last! Give Myshella up to me."

A cunning expression came over the sorcerer's face. "No. Destroy me and she is also destroyed. Beings of Pio—turn your full strength against Tanelorn. Raze it utterly and show this fool what we can do!"

Each of the reptilian riders directed their oddly shaped weapons at Tanelorn where Rackhir, Moonglum and the rest waited on the battlements.

"No!" shouted Elric. "You cannot—"

There was something flashing on the battlements. They were unfurling at last the banners of bronze. And as each banner was unfurled a pure golden light blazed out from it until there was a vast wall of light stretching the whole length of the defences, making it impossible to see the banners themselves or the men who held them. The beings of Pio aimed their weapons and released streams of fire at the barrier of light which immediately repelled them.

Theleb K'aarna's face was suffused with anger. "What is this? Our earthly sorcery cannot stand against the power of Pio!"

Elric smiled savagely. "This is not our sorcery—it is another sorcery which *can* resist that of Pio! Now, Theleb K'aarna, give up Myshella!"

"No! You are not protected as Tanelorn is protected. Beings of Pio—destroy him!"

And, as the weapons began to be directed at him, Elric flung the first of the arrows of quartz. It flew true—directly into the face of the leading reptilian rider. A high whining escaped the rider's throat as it raised its webbed hands towards the arrow embedded in its eye. The beast the rider sat upon reared, for it was plain that it was only barely controlled. It turned away from the blinding light from Tanelorn and it galloped at earth-shaking speed away into the desert, the dead rider falling from its back. A streak of fire barely missed Elric and he was forced to take the bird up higher, flinging down another arrow and seeing it strike a rider's heart. Again the mount went out of control and followed its companion into the desert. But there were ten more of the riders and each now turned his weapon against Elric, though finding it hard to aim as all the mounts grew restive and sought to accompany the two who had fled. Elric left it to the metal bird to duck and to dive through the criss-cross of beams and he hurled down another arrow and another. His clothes and his hair were singed and he remembered another time when he had ridden the bird across the Boiling Sea. Part of the bird's right wing-tip had been melted and its flight was a little more erratic. But still it climbed and dived and still Elric threw the arrows of quartz into the ranks of the beings of Pio. Then, suddenly, there were only two left and they were turning to flee, for nearby a cloud of unpleasant blue smoke had begun to erupt where Theleb K'aarna had been. Elric flung the last arrows after the reptiles of Pio and took each rider in the back. Now there were only corpses upon the sand.

The blue smoke cleared and Theleb K'aarna's horse stood there. And there was another corpse revealed. It was that of Myshella, Empress of the Dawn, and her throat had been cut. Theleb K'aarna had vanished, doubtless with the aid of sorcery.

Sickened, Elric descended on the bird of metal. On the walls of Tanelorn the light faded. He dismounted and he saw that the bird was weeping dark tears from its emerald eyes. He knelt beside Myshella.

An ordinary mortal could not have done it, but now she opened her lips and she spoke, though blood bubbled from her mouth and her words were hard to make out.

"Elric . . ."

"Can you live?" Elric asked her. "Have you some power to . . ."

"I cannot live. I am slain. Even now I am dead. But it will be some comfort to you to know that Theleb K'aarna has earned the disdain of the great Chaos Lords. They will never aid him again as they aided him this time, for in their eyes he has proved himself incompetent."

"Where has he gone? I will pursue him. I will slay him the next time, that I swear."

"I think that you will. But I do not know where he went. Elric—I am dead and my work is threatened. I have fought against Chaos for centuries and now, I think, Chaos will increase its power. Soon the great battle between the Lords of Law and the Lords of Entrophy will take place. The threads of destiny become much tangled—the very structure of the universe seems about to transform itself. You have some part in this . . . some part. . . . Farewell, Elric!"

"Oh, Myshella!"

"Is she dead now?" It was the sombre voice of the bird of metal.

"Aye." The word was forced from Elric's tight throat.

"Then I must take her back to Kaneloon."

Gently Elric picked up Myshella's bloody corpse, supporting the half-severed head on his arm. He placed the body in the onyx saddle.

The bird said: "We shall not see each other again, Prince Elric, for my death shall follow closely upon Lady Myshella's."

Elric bowed his head.

The shining wings spread and, with the sound of cymbals clashing, beat at the air.

Elric watched the beautiful creature circle in the sky, and then turn and fly steadily towards the south and World's Edge.

He buried his face in his hands, but he was beyond weeping now. Was it the fate of all the women he loved to die? Would Myshella have lived if she had let him die when he had wanted to? There was no rage left in him, only a sense of impotent despair.

He felt a hand on his shoulder and he turned. Moonglum stood there, with Rackhir beside him. They had ridden out from Tanelorn to find him.

"The banners have vanished," Rackhir told him. "And the arrows, too. Only the corpses of those creatures remain and we shall bury them. Will you come back with us, now, to Tanelorn?"

"Tanelorn cannot give me peace, Rackhir."

"I believe that to be true. But I have a potion in my house which will deaden some of your memories, help you forget some of what has happened lately."

"I would be grateful for such a potion. Though I doubt . . ."

"It will work. I promise. Another would achieve

complete forgetfulness from drinking this potion. But you may hope to forget a little."

Elric thought of Corum and Erekosë and Jhary-a-Conel and the implications of his experiences—that even if he were to die he would be reincarnated in some other form to fight again and to suffer again. An eternity of warfare and of pain. If he could forget that knowledge it would be enough. He had the impulse to ride far away from Tanelorn and concern himself as much as he could in the pettier affairs of men.

"I am so weary of gods and their struggles," he murmured as he mounted his golden mare.

Moonglum stared out into the desert.

"But when will the gods themselves weary of it, I wonder?" he said. "If they did, it would be a happy day for Man. Perhaps all our struggling, our suffering, our conflicts are merely to relieve the boredom of the Lords of the Higher Worlds. Perhaps that is why when they created us they made us imperfect."

They began to ride towards Tanelorn while the wind blew sadly across the desert. The sand was already beginning to cover up the corpses of those who had sought to wage war against eternity and had, inevitably, found that other eternity which was death.

For a while Elric walked his horse beside the others. His lips formed a name but did not speak it.

And then, suddenly, he was galloping towards Tanelorn dragging the screaming runesword from its scabbard and brandishing it at the impassive sky, making the horse rear up and lash its hooves in the air, shouting over and over again in a voice full of roaring misery and bitter rage:

"Ah, damn you! Damn you! Damn you!"

But those who heard him—and some might have been the Gods he addressed—knew that it was Elric of Melniboné himself who was truly damned.